Augustin F

Garrick's Pupil

Augustin Filon

Garrick's Pupil

1st Edition | ISBN: 978-3-75232-674-1

Place of Publication: Frankfurt am Main, Germany

Year of Publication: 2020

Outlook Verlag GmbH, Germany.

GARRICK'S PUPIL.

By AUGUSTIN FILON

CHAPTER I.

PAINTER AND MODEL.

Just as the third hour of the afternoon had sounded from the belfry of Saint Martin's-in-the-Fields, a hackney coach drew up before the most pretentious mansion upon the west side of Leicester Fields; and while the coachman hastened to agitate the heavy door-knocker, a young woman, almost a child, sprang out upon the pavement without waiting to have the shaky steps unfolded and lowered for her convenience. Her dust-colored mantle, disarranged by her rapid movements, revealed a rich costume beneath; while the dazzled passer-by might have caught a glimpse, amidst the whiteness of the elevated skirts, of a tiny pair of red satin slippers and two slender, exquisitely moulded ankles finely clad in silken hose with embroidered clocks.

The girl turned and assisted a more aged woman, leaning upon a crutch-headed cane, to descend. This lady wore the big straw bonnet and gray gown of the Quaker persuasion,—a rigidly simple costume, which occasionally is becoming to extreme youth, but rarely enhances maturer charms.

It was one of those glorious days of the English springtide when life seems endurable even to the hapless, grateful even to the invalid. A bland breeze rustled the branches of the grand old trees which in double rows framed the open square. Several children were at play upon the spacious grass-plot, which was intersected by diagonal paths of yellow sand. The square was silent, and slept in the voluptuous warmth of the perfect afternoon; but from the north side came the bustle and confusion that resembled the turmoil of some festival. It was the continuous din of the two tides of life which here meet and cross each other, the one surging from Covent Garden and Chancery Lane, the other from Piccadilly and St. James's. Pedestrians and horsemen, coaches and sedan chairs, went to make up a glittering, varied hodgepodge, amidst which flower-girls and newsboys fought their way, together with the venders of "hot buns." Gentlemen saluted with exaggerated gesture, pressing their cocked hats to their breasts and affectedly inclining their heads towards their right shoulder; while the ladies fluttered their fans and nodded the edifices of flowers and feathers which served in lieu of a head-dress. The intoxicating odor of iris powder, of benzoin, bergamot, and patchouli floated upon the air. The beggars leaning against the railing of the square and the Irish chairmen indolently smoking their pipes, for whom life is but a spectacle, watched the passage of others' happiness. A bright, genial sun polished the flanks of the plaster horse in the centre of the square, upon which rode a prince of the House of Hanover. It shone upon the head of the gilded cock which served as sign to Hogarth's old shop, flamed upon the windows of Newton's sham observatory, glistened upon the roofs, played along the line of coaches, set tiny mirrors upon the harnesses of the horses, glittered in the diamonds in the women's ears, and on the swords that clattered against the men's legs, set a spangle here or a spark there, and bathed all things in a blaze of light and joy.

Meanwhile a lackey in a livery embroidered in silver had opened the door to the two women.

"Sir Joshua Reynolds?"

The lackey hesitated, but at the moment Ralph, the painter's confidential man, appeared upon the steps.

"Miss Woodville?" he inquired in his turn.

"Yes," replied the girl.

"Be good enough to follow me, Miss Woodville"; adding with a smile, "You are prompt."

"It is the custom of the theatre. Lean upon my arm, aunt."

At this moment Miss Woodville was saluted with a "good-morning" uttered by so strange, so guttural, so piercing a voice that she involuntarily started.

"Don't be alarmed," said Ralph; "it is the bird."

"What bird?"

"Sir Joshua's parrot. He was in the courtyard, but had to be removed to the dining-room because he fought with the eagle."

"An eagle! a parrot! Pray what are they doing here?"

"They pose. Miss Woodville must have noticed them in more than one of Sir Joshua's pictures. Oh, we all take our turns in sitting as models to him. Yesterday I was a shepherd; the day before, a sea-god."

The good man drew himself up at the recollection of the lofty dignity with which his master's confidence had invested him.

Thus chatting, they reached the first floor. Ralph introduced the ladies into a gallery filled with roughly sketched canvases. He knocked twice upon the door at the extreme end, but received no response.

"How deaf the President grows!" he murmured, shaking his head.

Without further delay he opened the door.

Miss Woodville and her companion found themselves upon the threshold of quite a spacious chamber, lighted by a large window facing the north and nine feet in height.

The room contained an easel upon which rested a white canvas; near the easel stood a large mirror; upon a table near by lay the palette, all ready and fresh, with a row of little paint jars. The model's chair, raised upon a dais and revolving upon a pivot, was placed next to that of the painter, and opposite the mirror. About the room several sofas were arranged. There were no knickknacks; no cluttering; nothing to offend the sight, unless it was that just about the painter's chair the floor was black with snuff.

The man who advanced slowly to meet the strangers, making use of his maul-stick as a cane, while in the other he carried a silver ear-trumpet, was none other than Sir Joshua Reynolds himself, the greatest painter of women that the world has ever known.

The first impression he made upon his visitors was disappointing, indefinable.

That expansive brow which the hair, brushed straightly back, disclosed did not lack nobility; but the under lip, cleft by a wound and shrunken in the middle, lent to the mouth an expression at once unpleasant and strained. The eyes were concealed behind the crystalline glimmer of spectacles securely attached to the back of the head by broad black ribbons. The spare, calmly cold figure bore neither the trace of precise age nor the certainty of sex. At some distance and in obscurity one would have hesitated to pronounce it as that of a youth or an aged woman. Perhaps in some way the air of indecision and anxiety was due to that expression peculiar to those afflicted with deafness whose aim it is to dissimulate their infirmity.

He cast upon the old Quakeress a rapid, searching glance; then his eyes rested complacently upon Miss Woodville; his features, cold to unpleasantness, softened and became animated. Already had he painted three thousand portraits, but, far from being weary of his profession, his enthusiasm for the wonders of the human physiognomy increased each time that he found himself in the presence of a new model. Each time he thought, "*This* will be my *chef-d'œuvre*!"

The girl was quickly relieved of her mantle, which Ralph laid aside. She was dressed in the costume of Rosalind, as she had appeared at Drury Lane for the first time six months previously,—memorable night! when she had only to show herself to vanquish and carry by storm the hearts of all London.

A wide-brimmed hat of gray felt with plumes, a corsage of rose-pink taffety embroidered in silver, and a skirt of green velvet closely plaited—such was the costume.

The small, childish head, framed in a profusion of chestnut curls, was illumined by a pair of great brown eyes. With the eye of a connoisseur Reynolds regarded the delicate complexion, over which ran at the slightest provocation the rosiest of blushes, and over which every throb of the heart sent a hint of the tide of life, regarded that brilliant, mobile glance of the eye, in the depths of which played every description of piqued curiosity and *naïf* desire, lost in the riotous joy of living, of being sweet sixteen, celebrated and beautiful.

"Sit there, Miss Woodville," said the President of the Royal Academy, indicating the pivot chair.

"What! Ought I not to be placed opposite you?"

"No; rather at my side. We shall both benefit by the arrangement. Instead of looking at an ugly old painter, you will perceive your own charming image in the mirror and will smile upon it, while I have my sketch all done for me."

The old lady had drawn a roll of bank-notes from her pocket, which she proceeded carefully to count and re-count.

"I believe it is the custom," she said.

Sir Joshua acquiesced in silence with a cold smile. An able accountant and serious man of business, this President of the Royal Academy! The price of his portraits was invariably paid him, one half on the occasion of the first sitting, the remainder on the day that the finished work was delivered. As to the price, it varied according to the dimension; it had also varied with the epoch and had increased with the reputation of the artist. A full-length portrait cost at that time (1780) one hundred and fifty pounds sterling.

The Quakeress, therefore, placed upon a table seventy-five pounds in notes and gold pieces bearing the effigy of George III. As Miss Woodville was not yet sufficiently wealthy to order a portrait from the great painter, a group of enthusiastic amateurs had raised the necessary money in order to decorate the lobby of the theatre with the portrait.

"Am I permitted to talk?" inquired the girl.

"As much as you please."

"Oh, that's good!" she said, drawing a breath of relief; "and may I ask a question?"

"Ten, if you see fit."

"Sir Joshua, why are you making me so deathly white? I look like a statue."

Reynolds smiled.

"What will you say at the next sitting? I shall tint you all in Naples yellow."

"Fie!—horrors! Why do you do that?"

"Ah, that is my little secret! My enemies pretend that I have scraped a Watteau, others say a Titian, in order to discover the successive layers of color and surprise the method of these masters. And why should I not? All means are justifiable so long as one succeeds in imitating life. Others pretend that I paint on wax. They may say what they please. Hudson, my master, painted exceedingly well on cheese."

"On cheese!" exclaimed Miss Woodville with a laugh; "fancy a painting on cheese!"

"Exactly so."

Thereupon ensued a pause, during which the canvas was heard to crack beneath the pencil, while the old lady's needles clicked where she sat knitting. Evidently ill at ease, Reynolds fretted upon his chair. At last he turned towards the Quakeress and courteously remarked, "The time will hang heavily upon your hands, madam."

"I have brought my work, and have no end of patience," she replied.

"That may be; but the first sitting is always tedious. Moreover, I need to become intimately acquainted with my model, and since Miss Woodville does not play this evening, I count upon keeping your niece for supper, if you have no objection. I am to have a few friends here, for whom my sister will do the honors as hostess,—Mr. Burke, Dr. Johnson, my charming neighbor, Miss Burney."

"The author of 'Evelina'! Oh, I long to meet her!"

"So you see, madam, you may spare yourself a tedious wait, and without fear leave Miss Woodville in my care. I shall make it my duty to see that she is returned to you properly escorted."

Thus politely dismissed, the old lady regretfully arose, but seemed still to hesitate.

"Go, aunt, or you will miss the reunion of 'The Favorites of Jesus Christ,' of whom you are the presiding officer," suggested the younger lady.

Whether influenced by this consideration, or whether she found it difficult to resist the desire which the painter had so delicately expressed, the Quakeress retired, escorted even to the threshold by Sir Joshua.

"Are you aware," he asked, returning to his model, "of my true purpose in sending this lady away?"

"In truth, no."

"Because she constrains you; because she casts a shadow upon your youth and gayety; in a word, because she prevents you from being yourself."

"Pray, how could you divine that?"

"My dear child, I have already deciphered three thousand human visages, and why should I not have learned to read the soul a little? The lady is your aunt?"

"Yes,—at least I have been told to call her so."

"And your parents?"

"My mother is dead; I never knew her. My father has travelled for the past fifteen years in foreign lands; perhaps I shall never see him. While a mere child I was placed in Miss Hannah More's boarding-school at Bristol. One day we learned that our mistress was a poetic genius, that Dr. Johnson himself had deigned to encourage her. You cannot imagine, Sir Joshua, what a sensation the tidings created among us girls! We all sighed to compose verse —or to recite. It was discovered that I spoke rather better than the others. I swear to you that I was possessed of but one desire,—to appear in costume, to escape from that frightful gray gown and that horrible Quaker bonnet in which we were all hooded. One day I was made to declaim before Mr. Garrick. He wished to give me lessons and make an actress of me. And a few months later I made my *début*."

"And a genuine triumph it was! I was there."

"It was then that I was informed that I had an aunt, a sister of my mother, and I was forthwith placed in her care, in her guardianship."

"And she has rigorously acquitted herself of the mission which was confided to her."

The child heaved a deep sigh.

"Ah, Sir Joshua! It is not that she is unkind in any way, but she is my constant shadow. In the wings, in the greenroom, at the rehearsals, she is ever at my side, answering questions which are put to me, refusing invitations, reading letters which are addressed to me, and forcing me to sing psalms to put to rout the evil thoughts which I find in Shakespeare!"

"I see; and you long to be free?"

"Oh, yes, passionately!"

"And what use would you make of your liberty?"

"Oh, I can't fancy. Perhaps I might love virtue if it were not crammed down my throat."

"Good!"

"But you do not know the worst yet."

"Well?"

"The worst—is Reuben!"

"And who may Reuben be?"

"My cousin, my aunt's son; but he is no Quaker. He belongs to one of those old, rigid, cruel sects which have been perpetuated in shadow since the days of the Puritans. He is a fanatic; it would rejoice his heart to plunge into a sea of papist blood; meanwhile he torments me."

"Perhaps he loves you?"

"Yes, according to his light, which surely is not a fair light."

"And what is the proper method of loving?"

The girl burst into a coquettish laugh.

"You ask me more than I can tell, Sir Joshua."

"Indeed? Pray how, then, can one who is ignorant of the sentiment impart its faithful presentment to others? How can she communicate an emotion which finds no echo in her own soul? Who has the ability to teach her to invest her voice, her gestures, her glance, her very smile, with the woes and joys of love?"

"Garrick, I tell you!"

That name, cast haphazard into their conversation, caused a divergence.

"Poor Garrick!" exclaimed Reynolds ruefully; "it is scarcely yet a year since we left him alone in his glory beneath the pavement of Westminster."

The mobile countenance of the child actress reflected as a mirror the sad memory evoked by the artist; a tear glistened upon the lashes of her beautiful eyes.

"He was your friend?" she inquired.

"Oh, yes; one of whom I was very proud."

"Did you paint his portrait?"

"Many times. He posed marvellously, and never tormented me as he did one of my fellow-artists to whom quite unwillingly he had accorded some sittings."

"What did he do?"

"Changed his mask every five minutes, until the poor artist, believing that he as often had a new model before him, or the devil, perhaps, flung away his brushes in despair."

"Garrick once told me," said Esther Woodville, "that the son of a friend, recently dead, had sought him to complain of some trickery by which he had been deprived of a portion of his inheritance. A certain old man, to whom the deceased had intrusted a considerable sum, denied the trust and refused to make restitution. Do you know what Garrick did? Arrayed in the attire of the dead, he played the ghost, and played it so well that the wretch, terrified beyond measure, made confession and restored the property."

"I never heard the anecdote; it is curious," said Reynolds, taking a pinch of snuff.

He extended the open box to the actress, but she refused it with a slight grimace.

"You make a mistake," he said; "this is some 37, Hardham's; our *élégantes* prefer it to any other." Then after a brief pause he added, "Your physiognomy is scarcely less changeable than Garrick's; you have laughed, you have wept; you have been gay, excited, mournful. Now, of all these expressions which have chased each other over your charming face—nay, do not blush; I am an old man—of all these varied expressions which is the veritable, the dominant one,—the one which expresses the character of your soul? As long as I fail to discover this expression in the model, so long is my brush paralyzed. I am obliged to seek until I find it. I have painted Garrick both in tragedy and comedy; Admiral Keppel, sword in hand, upon the point of giving the order to clear the decks for action; Kitty Fisher, at her toilet, since it was her profession to be beautiful and to please. I have represented Goldsmith writing the final pages of the 'Vicar' or the sweet verses of the 'Deserted Village'; Sterne, thinking of poor Maria's suffering or of the death of Lieut. Lefèvre. His wig was all awry and the rascal wanted to straighten it. 'Let it be as it is!' I said to him; 'if it is straight, you are no longer the author of 'Tristram Shandy.' When I paint a child I give it some playthings; a young mother, I surround her with her children. Notice this one, for instance—"

"That is my comrade, Mrs. Hartley."

"Exactly. She carries her little daughter upon her back and laughs merrily. Fanciful maternity! There are mythological beauties and modern beauties.

The one will be a nymph and gently rest her limbs upon the velvet sward in the genial atmosphere of a Grecian landscape; the other, muffled up to her neck, her muff pressed to her nose, in order to conceal a mouth that is a trifle expansive, elects to promenade the denuded paths of her park and leave the imprint of her tiny, fur-clad feet along the snow. It is the cold, you understand, which lends brilliancy to the eyes and a rosy tip to the ear; it is the cold that gives color and life. Thus I strive to place every human being in his or her favorite attitude, amidst congenial surroundings, beneath the ray which is best calculated to illumine. And I lie in wait for the divine moment when the woman exhales all her seduction, the man all the power of his mind."

He paused for a moment.

"Well, and you!" he continued quickly. "I have not found you yet; I have no hold upon you. I must attempt some subterfuge."

Thereupon he raised his voice.

"Frank!—Frank!"

A masked door, which Esther had not remarked, opened almost immediately and a young man of perhaps two and twenty years of age appeared upon the threshold. Miss Woodville uttered a stifled cry and half rose from her chair.

"My lord!" she breathed almost inaudibly; "how comes it that—you—"

"I see how it is!" remarked Sir Joshua; "you are the dupe of a resemblance. Your gaze is not resting upon Lord Mowbray, but upon my apprentice, Francis Monday. My dear Frank, be good enough to fall upon your knees before this fair young woman and look at her as if you adored her."

Pallid, mute, with lips tightly compressed, Frank stood motionless.

"I, Sir Joshua?" he faltered. "You wish me to—"

"Certainly! Now, then!"

With evident effort the young man slowly advanced as if he were going to execution. Beads of perspiration pearled upon his brow. Nevertheless, disturbed though he was, the beauty of his features and the innate nobility of his person prevented any awkwardness of carriage. With drooping eyelids he fell upon his knees at the girl's feet, while at the moment, as if actuated by some invincible power, he raised his glance full of a desperate passion. Truly, for a timid boy taken unawares, Frank played the comedy of love like a consummate master.

A rosy blush suffused Esther's features, entirely irradiating them, as a summer's sunrise illumines the delicious purity of the dawn. Astonishment, shame, pleasure, malice, every shade of sentiment was in an instant born, in an instant expired, fading in a most ravishing *mélange*. With head slightly inclined, bosom heaving, eyelids trembling, and lips quivering, her whole being vibrated in unison with the precipitate throbbing of her heart.

"Rosalind listening to Orlando's declaration!" exclaimed Sir Joshua. "I have it! The portrait is assured! I have no further need of you, Frank."

The young man rose, his eyes still fixed upon Esther; then without a word he directed his steps towards the masked door which had afforded him access to the studio and vanished.

By slow degrees the blush which had invaded the girl's cheeks and brow faded until not a vestige remained.

CHAPTER II.

A SUPPER AT SIR JOSHUA'S.

The company assembled in the Reynolds's drawing-room when the artist entered, leading Miss Woodville by the hand, made such a palaver over the young actress that it was quite enough to turn her head, had she not already become accustomed to clamorous triumphs. She found herself in the arms of three women at once, who emulously cajoled her, while the men vied with them in paying flattering court. Despite her *aplomb*, spoiled child that she was, she was becoming quite embarrassed in responding to all the hand-pressures, the smiling eyes, the gracious questions, when, fortunately for her, a footman announced supper; and forthwith the company passed into the dining-room.

It was just five o'clock, and, being well aware of the rules of the house, Sir Joshua's guests were all present, even in greater number than was expected, as was frequently the case. On this account some little confusion prevailed about the table, where each one seated himself according to his fancy. There were not enough plates; one person possessed a fork but no knife, while another was furnished with a knife minus a fork: but at these gay, free-and-easy reunions such trifles were passed over with a laugh. The master of the house, whose special delight it was to chat with his guests, fluttered from one to the other, ear-trumpet in hand, giving the entertainment not the slightest heed. Miss Reynolds alone was in despair.

In point of fact, Miss Reynolds never appeared in any other attitude. A genuine martyr was Miss Reynolds. Martyr to whom or what? It would be difficult to explain. Following the example of her brother, she painted, but, although she was the sister of a great artist, to her profound surprise her pictures were detestable. Sir Joshua owned a great gilded coach, upon the panels of which Hayman had painted the Seasons, but he rarely availed himself of its comforts; instead, he obliged his sister to drive out in it, and used to send her to the park "for the good of her health." And the passers-by were astonished to see, shrinking in a corner of the resplendent equipage, a woman who wept scalding tears. It was Miss Reynolds, the everlasting martyr. Upon this particular occasion she exerted herself to the last degree without producing the slightest effect either upon her guests or her domestics.

In the midst of the excitement a woman of perhaps thirty years, arrayed in a peach-bloom gown and a head-dress of lace, quickly approached Esther. She was beautiful, of slender elegance, with eyes full of fire, and cheeks of a violent tint; she spoke in a high-pitched key, and altogether exhibited the assurance of a high-born lady. She promptly pounced upon the girl and dragged her away with her.

"Miss Woodville, dear Miss Woodville! I want to be your friend! Sit here, close to me."

And she murmured, with a singular mixture of affectation and passion,—

"How lovely she is! Do you know, little one, that we shall positively be obliged to institute a body-guard, like my friends, Lady Coventry and Lady Waldegrave, who go about everywhere escorted by two officers and a dozen halberdiers to keep the crowd of their admirers at a distance?"

Esther leaned towards her neighbor, a man of middle age, whose extraordinary plainness of feature rendered him in a way sympathetic and assuring. Of him she inquired the name of the lady who so burned to be her intimate friend. She learned that it was Lady Vereker, one of the most pronounced women of the world of the period. In her turn Lady Vereker hastened to inform Esther in a whisper that her neighbor was Mr. Gibbon, quite an obscure member of Parliament and a commissioner of trade.

"It is said that he has written a great work upon the Romans," added Lady Vereker maliciously, "but to my thinking he does not look capable of it."

In fact, Mr. Gibbon was paying his fair neighbor too assiduous court to please her ladyship.

As no introductions were offered at Reynolds's house, in order to avoid ceremonies of which fashionable persons were more weary than the rest of the world, Esther knew none of the guests, and would have continued in ignorance had not Mr. Gibbon named them; and he accompanied each name with some neat, incisive, mocking little phrase, the secret of which he had learned during his sojourn in France.

"That great solemn figure is Mr. Burke," he explained. "He is vastly eloquent; a huge merit in Parliament, but a sad fault at supper. He shares his solicitude between Miss Burney and his son Richard. He idolizes the boy and never loses sight of him; notice that at this moment his arm is about his neck. He makes it his constant boast that this boy will be a genius. For my part I doubt it. The Phœnix never repeats himself!"

"But who is that strange personage seated on the other side of Miss Burney,— the man with the monstrous head that keeps rolling from shoulder to shoulder, with the twisted and seamed lips, and with eyes both of which are never open at the same moment? Why, his face is a positive grimace! He only succeeds in putting into his mouth half the contents of his plate; and he does not drink, he precipitates the liquid into his throat, and the descending nourishment is in a constant struggle with the ascending words. He disgusts and frightens me, while at the same time he attracts and interests. I am almost tempted to fall in love with him!"

"Brava! There is a portrait which would do credit to our amphitryon. The man is the one whom Chesterfield dubbed the respectable Hottentot; he is the dictator of the republic of letters; in a word, it is Dr. Johnson. That poor man whom you see, with straining eyes and ear bent towards the Doctor, gathering the lightest word which falls from his lips, and who will hand him down to posterity some day, is Boswell, his friend, his fag, and his disciple. The man who is a disciple—a genuine one, I mean—alone has sounded the depths of human folly. Perhaps it is Boswell who has taught Johnson to despise men, and it is Boswell who will teach men to admire Johnson. Now, just beyond Lady Vereker sits Mr. Hanway, whose profile only is visible."

"And who is Mr. Hanway?"

"Very much of a fool in a good sense,—no rare virtue in this isle of ours. He has written upon finance, peace, war, music, ventilation, the poor, Canada; upon military diet, the police, prisons, chimney-sweeps, and God Almighty."

"Is that all?" asked Esther with a laugh.

"I believe so, though he is capable of discovering no end of topics, since his device is, Never despair. He has imported from Persia, where he encountered infinite dangers, a certain very curious machine,—a little roof of colored silk extended upon ribs of whalebone, secured in turn to a rod of iron, and which is carried about at the end of a long handle as a protection against the rain. It is called an umbrella."

"What an odd idea!"

"In order to habituate people to the sight and usage of his instrument, Hanway selects rainy days for his perambulations, when he can spread his portable tent. The children throw mud at him and the serving maids laugh. It is free sport to try to crush his umbrella. They make all manner of fun of him, but perhaps it is wrong, since the folly of to-day is the wisdom of to-morrow."

At last Esther knew all the guests. Mr. Gibbon had named them all, except one whose name she did not inquire.

Seated at the extremity of the room, Frank every now and then allowed his sad, unfathomable eyes to wander towards the girl. Indifferent to all that was uttered about him, his melancholy contrasted powerfully with the joyous air which every face wore. Even though she smiled at Mr. Gibbon's quips and responded to the lively, caressing words of Lady Vereker, Miss Woodville was conscious of the espionage, and the sentiment it evoked was not displeasing to her.

The conversation became general, often rising far above whispered particularities. War became the topic, and the latest news from America. It was said that the savages who were fighting with the English had killed and eaten some American colonists, and not one of the European generals had raised a hand to stay the barbarity. A caricature, exposed at Humphrey's, depicted George III. taking part in the frightful orgy and disputing possession of a bone with an Indian chief.

"It is horrible!" cried Miss Burney; "our poor king has nothing whatever to do with it, but how can English gentlemen ally themselves with these cannibals?"

The casual mention of Cape Breton in the conversation reminded Mr. Burke of an anecdote. Every one present lapsed into silence to hear it.

"Indolent as may be our masters of to-day," he said, "they will never equal the sloth and ignorance of the late Duke of Newcastle. You cannot imagine his astonishment when one day some one informed him that Cape Breton was an island. 'A cape an island!' he exclaimed; 'I am amazed. I really must tell the king. He will be vastly diverted!' This man would have sacrificed cities and provinces without so much as a thought. But what mattered it to him, so long as he was minister!"

"Our own are not much better than he," remarked one of the guests; "they have disgraced Admiral Keppel, the only man to-day who is able to sweep the seas of the French and Spaniards."

"Bah! Rodney is worth twenty Keppels."

"Rodney! a blusterer! Have you heard of his adventure with Maréchal de Biron?"

"No; what is it?"

"He had taken refuge from his creditors in France and was dining at the Marshal's table. 'Ah,' he remarked, 'were it not for my debts I would return and would destroy your fleet until not one of your vessels remained.'— 'Monsieur,' replied the Maréchal, 'pray do not let that deter you. Your debts are paid. Go and fight us—if you can!' That was three years ago; Rodney commands our fleet, thanks to the friendship of Lord Sandwich, and the naval power of our enemies is still intact!"

From this grand topic the conversation suddenly changed to the discussion of worldly amusements upon which the war had had no effect. They spoke of the last success of Siddons. Upon the queen of tragedy, as upon Admiral Rodney, there was, although the political question had amounted to nothing, a confused mixture of opinions which clashed and provoked comment.

"She is adorable!"

"A leaden idol, your Siddons!"

Next they discussed Pacchierotti, the famous Italian tenor, and his approaching *début* in a new *rôle*. Then they spoke of the new books. Some one at the table mentioned the word "bluestocking." The expression was a novelty at the time, and created a sensation.

"Don't allude to bluestockings in my presence!" cried the author of "Evelina," making a shield of her fan.

"You a bluestocking!" exclaimed Burke indignantly. "There is no bluestocking where there is no leaven of pedantry. Now, if it were a question of poor Mrs. Carpenter."

"Yes," interposed Gibbon, "the ill-starred lady has translated Epictetus!"

"And Mrs. Cholmondeley,—do you give her a place among the bluestockings?"

"She's too great a woman for that!"

"I was at her house yesterday," remarked Miss Burney; "I found her very affable."

"Affability," muttered Dr. Johnson, "is the first lieutenant of pride."

In hot haste Boswell produced his tablets from his pocket in order to note the aphorism which had fallen from the oracle's lips.

"I find Mrs. Thrale a worthy person," remarked Gibbon, "and an agreeable mistress of her house."

"The wife of a brewer?" inquired Lady Vereker, with just a hint of disdain in her tone.

"A most intelligent woman!" retorted Miss Burney; "she has saved her husband from ruin."

"But it appears that she has not preserved him from another accident," replied Lady Vereker languidly.

The guests were beginning to indulge in a smile, when suddenly Dr. Johnson's formidable head began to oscillate, while from his chair emanated a cracking sound of evil augury. Until this moment he had remained silent, breathing heavily between his closely set teeth as if trying to imitate the hiss of a saw, meanwhile enveloping his neighbor, Miss Burney, with a glance of grotesque tenderness in which paternal interest struggled with love; but at the sarcasm of Lady Vereker against his friend, Mrs. Thrale, he bridled and assumed his attitude of combat. "Madam!" he burst forth in a voice of thunder, and there he paused like Hercules with club poised in air.

"The bolt is about to fall," whispered Gibbon.

An atmosphere of apprehension prevailed about the table. Lady Vereker alone, with an intrepid though somewhat pallid smile, raised her pretty head with charming effrontery to brave the blow. But it was Fate's decree that the bolt should not fall, and that the Doctor should not be heard from that evening. Just at the moment that his lips parted to avenge the honor of Mrs. Thrale, the door opened to admit Ralph. With a fluttered air he hastened to his master and whispered a word or two in his ear.

Sir Joshua was upon his feet in an instant.

"Gentlemen," he cried, "great news! It appears that we have calumniated Rodney! He has completely routed the Spanish fleet under Admiral Langara. Five vessels are captured; one is blown up and the rest dispersed! Rodney has washed his hands of one half of his engagement to Maréchal de Biron. Permit me to propose the health of Admiral Rodney!"

Naturally Burke, like his friend Reynolds, would have preferred to drink to the health of Keppel; but patriotism proved more potent than party spirit. All the guests rose to drink the proposed toast, and the repast ended as it had begun,—in a sort of joyous tumult. Thereupon they left the table, and each one went his way in pursuit of pleasure or business,—Reynolds to the academy, Burke to Parliament; Johnson and Boswell wended their way to the "Turk's Head," that taproom where literary folk were wont to meet. Mr. Gibbon offered his arm to Miss Burney to escort her to her father's house, Dr. Burney, who lived near by at the head of St. Martin's Street; while Lady Vereker declared that she would permit no one but herself the pleasure of seeing Miss Woodville home to her aunt.

"I shall carry you away!" she said in a decided way which would not have been out of place upon the lips of a veritable cavalier.

Her ladyship's little black page, arrayed in a rich Oriental costume of crimson embroidered in gold, ran before them to lower the carriage steps. The majestic Hungarian chamberlain doffed his plumed hat and smote the pavement with his tall cane. The footmen, shaking their great epaulettes, quickly sprang to their posts and climbed to the back of the coach.

Upon entering the warmed and perfumed equipage, Esther descried two living forms moving about, two bundles of flesh and hair in ribbons, which sprang upon Lady Vereker.

"Wait a moment!" said she; "permit me to present you.—Bambino, my monkey; Spadillo, my favorite dog. The former comes from Barbadoes, the latter from Vigo. Pray notice that they wear my colors. I adore them both, and I would refuse to go anywhere, even to Paradise, without Bambino and Spadillo."

At that moment the horses started off with much pawing and champing, and simultaneously the eyes of the two women fell upon Francis Monday, who stood upon the threshold of the mansion, bowing to them with profound respect.

CHAPTER III.

LADY VEREKER'S BOUDOIR.

"He's not bad, that boy," said the *grande dame*, "Miss Reynolds has often told me how her brother found him in the street."

"Is it possible?"

"Yes. It's a queer story, but I have forgotten it. My memory is so unreliable!"

"The young man bears a remarkable resemblance to Lord Mowbray," ventured Esther thoughtfully.

Lady Vereker started brusquely and faced her companion so far as their relative positions in the carriage would permit.

"Are you acquainted with Lord Mowbray?" she demanded. "You have seen him, spoken with him? He loves you, perhaps?"

The queries succeeded each other with breathless speed, imperiously demanding a response; at the same time her ladyship had caught the girl's hands in her own as if to usurp her, to make her very volition prisoner. Simple curiosity used no such speech, such gestures. And she added, pressing Esther's fingers in her clasp:—

"The young girl who loves Lord Mowbray is lost!"

Ere Esther could make any reply a sudden check in the speed of the horses gave the carriage a violent shock. Miss Woodville uttered a cry of terror.

"What is it?" demanded Lady Vereker, lowering one of the windows.

"Please, your ladyship," replied the footman, touching his plumed hat, "the torches have frightened your ladyship's horses."

The two women looked out. The city presented an extraordinary aspect. Lanterns illuminated the fronts of the shops and the windows of the Tories, while those of the Whigs, closed, dark, and grim, protested against the joy of the rival party. Groups of men ran about, cheering and waving firebrands. Fires of boughs and waste lumber, saturated with pitch and turpentine, blazed at the street corners, while the children danced around them and the wayfarers approached to warm themselves; for a damp night had succeeded the beautiful day. In the dense volumes of smoke arose the pungent odor of resin and burning grease. The signs, hanging like iron flags from the long arms which stretched out almost into the middle of the street, shook in the wind with a rusty rattle and glittered here and there in the ruddy light.

"What is the matter?" cried Lady Vereker. "Oh, I recollect! Rodney! They are celebrating the Admiral's victory."

In fact, amidst the confused turmoil could be distinguished the name of Rodney mingled with cries of "Long live the peacemaker!" Indeed, the majority feared that this success would fail to create confidence in the ministers and thus prolong the war which they longed to put an end to at any cost.

"They say," continued the footman, "that the mob is about to burn Lord George Germaine and Lord North in effigy."

"My cousin!" said Lady Vereker with a laugh. "I should like to assist at that, and I would willingly place the first fagot on the pile!"

"It would not be prudent to go farther in this direction," said one of the footmen; "the crowd is very great, and if they were to recognize your ladyship's livery—"

"I see how it is," remarked Lady Vereker, still laughing, and turning to Esther; "the rascals are afraid. Very well; drive home by the shortest way. I shall be able to keep you a few minutes longer, my dear. Do not be anxious; a man shall be despatched to inform your friends that you are safe."

But Esther was not in the least disturbed. Was she not of that age when one blesses the slightest adventure that chances to disturb the monotonous course of every-day life and suddenly produces the unforeseen?

A few minutes later the two women were seated in one of those tiny, low-ceiled, over-decorated apartments in which the new instinct of intimacy and mystery confined the higher classes of the period. Louis XV. had first set the example of these miniature chambers which best suited the queens of his left hand. And all over Europe, where France still set the fashion, although she was the object of attack, every one strove to make a mystery of life, although in nine cases out of ten there was no reason for it. There were no longer the spacious galleries for state pageants, no longer the throne-like beds: but boudoirs round as nests and muffled in silken hangings; furniture monstrously stuffed, consoles and pier-tables, and *étagères* littered with costly nothings. Upon the walls, pastels and portraits of much-bedecked women, wearing the same vague, coquettish smile upon their vermilion lips. Not an angle was visible, and none of the straight-backed chairs which oblige the body to maintain a respectable position, but easy-chairs everywhere, into the depths of which one sank with voluptuous deliberation,—nothing but curves to invite ease and languor. The white woodwork and delicate, tender tints which had begun to prevail in France had not yet crossed the Channel. The day of the massive, so to speak, had passed; that of simplicity had not yet dawned. It was, in short, in the daintiest of boudoirs that Esther Woodville and her new friend drank tea out of exquisite Japanese cups. A fire crackled upon the hearth; a jet of water plashed softly as it fell into its marble basin at the feet of a nymph whose ideally slender limbs and elegant nudity were scarcely visible in the semi-obscurity that prevailed,—the image of the mistress of the house, by the celebrated Roubiliac, if we may credit indiscreet and envious tongues.

A silver lamp shed a mellow radiance upon the dainty and delicate objects which littered the table,—the *encas* always ready for my lady. The entire upper portion of the chamber, the panels painted by Lautherbourg, the azure ceiling where cupids sported, the marvellous great Venetian chandelier with its four hundred sparkling crystal drops,—all remained veiled in shadow, scarcely visible. A sweet but oppressive perfume, which seemed to exhale from everything, made the will languid and paralyzed the senses with a delicious stupor.

Lady Vereker had quitted her place and had taken a seat upon a tabouret close to Esther. She had captured one of the girl's hands and had riveted her gaze upon her face.

"You were saying," she began slowly, "that Lord Mowbray is in love with you."

"I said nothing of the kind. It was your ladyship who said so."

"In the first place, dear, drop 'your ladyship.' My name is Arabella. Those who love me call me Bella. Call me Bella, and I will call you Esther."

"I should not dare presume."

"Why not?"

"Such familiarity! and with one of your rank!"

"Of my age, you mean! A friend of twenty-eight years alarms one of sixteen, for you are sixteen, I believe."

"Seventeen," replied Esther with comical dignity.

"Well, I love you, and I want you to love me. Friendship is the true sentiment which unites women, the only one which relieves their delicacy of the fear of wounds, their devotion of treason. Oh, if I could but spare you some of the griefs of my life!"

"You have suffered?"

"Frightfully!" said Bella in a flippant tone which belied the tragic significance of the word. Then she continued:—

"Men are all wretches, but the worst one among them all is perhaps Lord Mowbray."

"What has he done?"

"He has accomplished everything that a man of his age can dream of in the way of forbidden and perverse actions. First, you must know that the late Lord Mowbray was the greatest libertine of his time. He was interested in that famous abbey of Medmonham with Lord Sandwich, Sir Francis Dashwood, and that abominable John Wilkes, the author of the 'Essay upon Woman,' whose soul is still more hideous than his visage. In their orgies they parodied the very ceremonies of religion. It is related that one day—one night, rather—Lord Sandwich administered the Holy Sacrament to a dog, carrying out the full rites."

"How horrible!" exclaimed Esther, clasping her hands.

"Is it not?" murmured Lady Vereker in the same tone; at the same time an imperceptible smile appeared in the corners of both pairs of lips.

"But let us leave the father in the abode for which he was certainly destined, and speak of the son. He has had as his instructor in vice his own tutor, a Frenchman named Lebeau, who took good care to ruin his pupil in early life, the better to master him later. It was in company with this man that he made the tour of Europe, stopping for the most part in France and Italy. He was but a mere boy when he grossly deceived the daughter of the clergyman at Mowbray Park. It is said, too, that he was the instigator and confidant of the first follies of the Prince of Wales. He is fiercely hated by the king, but especially so by the queen. He and his friends make it their boast that there is not an incorruptible woman in existence. Their debauchery differs from that of their fathers in that it is savored with villany. As formerly, these young gentlemen, who call themselves Mohawks, walk the streets at night with blackened faces, quarrel with inoffensive wayfarers, stop women, strip them and either beat or cast them naked into casks of pitch which they have placed beneath sheds, and laugh until they drown the cries of their victims. As for the watchmen, they prick their legs with their swords, bind them to the door-knockers, and oblige them to light the scene with their lanterns. These are only their malicious tricks, for they do worse. More than once they have profited by popular broils, or by the quarrels which have been common since the beginning of the war, to carry away young girls, and send a father, a husband, or a troublesome lover to the shades. It is said that they are responsible for many a death, and that if one should visit the 'Folly' which Mowbray possesses near Chelsea, if one were to sound the walls which are riddled with secret passages, if one should search the cellars which the Thames is made to inundate at certain hours, perhaps one would find the explanation of the desperate cries which have been heard by night in the silence of the country; perhaps one would discover human remains, skeletons cramped into attitudes which would tell the tale of the ferocity which had abused their last agony!"

In speaking thus this strange woman was completely transformed. Lately so flippant and sceptical, as were the women of her time, who scarcely ever spoke without an accompanying smile, she had become more tragic than Siddons. She spoke in a low, swift, sibilant tone close into Esther's face, filling her with fear, magnetizing her with her dark glance, and crushing her hands in her grip of iron almost without knowing it. Esther seemed quite terrified. Thereupon Bella resumed, in a soft, imploring voice,—

"And such is the man who pretends to love you, who perhaps makes your heart beat at this moment. But I will save you. Your embarrassment, your emotion, have told me their story. Have done with it all, and cast yourself upon the bosom of a true friend. Tell me all."

These final words, which ought to have assured Lady Vereker's victory, were just the ones which compromised her. Her eyes betrayed an all too anxious, too passionate desire to learn the truth! Like lightning a suspicion crossed Esther's mind: Does Lady Vereker love Lord Mowbray?

"You appear to know him exceedingly well," she said.

The words were uttered so unexpectedly that for a moment Bella was thrown off her guard. Her cleverly tinted face concealed her internal emotions, but a twitching of the lips, a rapid fluttering of the eyelids, did not escape Esther, who had become all at once dangerously keen, as is the case of every woman who suspects and wishes to know.

"She is lying!" thought Esther, though aloud she said:—

"Lord Mowbray was present at my *début*. As so many other gentlemen did, he sent me flowers, verses, and jewels; and—and that is all."

"She's lying!" thought Lady Vereker in her turn.

And both were correct. Lady Vereker forbore to tell Esther of the hold she had once had upon Lord Mowbray—a hold which she had not yet despaired of regaining, while Esther would not admit to Lady Vereker that she had rashly replied to one of Lord Mowbray's notes and already began to find it difficult to defend herself against his assiduities.

Without being the dupes of each other, but enlightened, the one by the experiences of life, the other by the precocious instinct of combat, the *comédienne* of the fashionable world and the *comédienne* of the theatre pressed each other's hands with tender interest and smiled amiably into each other's eyes.

CHAPTER IV.

THE BROOKS CLUB.

Eleven o'clock chimed from the tall clock placed opposite the fireplace. To its faint, silvery tones, which vibrated for some moments upon the atmosphere of the silent chamber, neighboring clocks, repeating the hour, seemed to make echo with their melancholy voices.

"Already eleven o'clock!" exclaimed Esther, starting to her feet. "I must go; I should be at home at this moment!"

"The crowd has not yet dispersed," answered Lady Vereker; "listen to their shouts."

Lady Vereker's mansion was situated upon Park Lane, at that day a lonesome part of the town, whither gentlemen were wont to come in the early morning to cross swords in order to get up an appetite, and instead frequently succeeded in turning their stomachs inside out. Bella approached one of the windows. Upon the faint, luminous grayness of the sky were sketched the outlines of Hyde Park wrapped in profound sleep, but the glow of the bonfires flushed the southern horizon, and from time to time savage outcries crossed the calmness of the night.

"They are delirious over their Rodney," said Bella with a shrug; "neither a chair nor a coach will be able to pass through St. James's, and the other side of the Green Park is deserted at this hour; we should risk being attacked there. Ah, me! how fortunate are common women! They can go everywhere. But why should we not change our attire? My women will accommodate us with gowns. *Pardieu!* that would be charming!"

Lady Vereker uttered her little oath in French. The idea of the masquerade pleased her immensely, and without waiting for Esther's acquiescence she began to put it in execution.

At the expiration of a quarter of an hour they were equipped as women of the lower class.

"Esther," exclaimed Lady Bella, "you look like a Soho dressmaker! And I, Fanchette, what do I look like?"

"I dare not say," replied the maid; "all that I can assure your ladyship is that in my gown you are—worse than I."

"Exactly as I desire to look," replied Lady Vereker with a burst of laughter at the impertinence.

Thereupon she started off, taking Esther by the arm, and forbidding even a footman to follow her. For that matter, her people seemed accustomed to the strange caprices of their mistress.

Upon reaching Piccadilly they passed suddenly from the shadow and silence into the tumult and violent glare of the bonfires. Many a joke was levelled at them as they passed. One man wearing clerical attire, and who seemed completely intoxicated, approached them, declaring that by Jupiter they were deucedly pretty girls and he would have a kiss from each! In order to escape him the two women ran down St. James Street, where the crowd separated them from the enterprising clergyman.

"A churchman!" panted Esther. "Can you believe it?"

"No, my dear: it was the Duke of Norfolk; he whom they call 'Jockey Norfolk.' His mania is for disguising himself as a country curate, and running about town and making a fool of himself. When he is dead-drunk people profit by his condition to rob him."

"What a horrible person!"

"On the contrary, I assure you that when he is sober he is most amiable."

In the neighborhood of St. James's the mob grew denser and more excited. There were beggar-women holding their new-born infants at arms' length, chairmen, sailors, thieves of all ages, recognizable by their skulking air and their sly, sharp glances, and finally a sprinkling of gentlemen, come hither after a good dinner to give vent to their political passions, or simply to amuse themselves by hustling the women and making a noise generally. The crowd laughed and vociferated, and threw stones at the windows of a grand mansion which belonged to one of the king's ministers. They applauded each successful shot, and howled over the failures.

At last all the ministerial windows were broken except one, which remained intact, protected by two caryatides which advanced like sentinels, supporting the roof; and against this single window were all the efforts directed, as if the detested minister were standing behind the sash, or as if the crushing of that bit of glass were going to cover the enemies of England with confusion and terminate the war at a blow.

The assailants excited each other by constantly crying, "Be bold, Tommy!" "At it again, Jack!" "Pluck up there, old boy!"

Suddenly a figure bounded from the midst of the crowd, a long arm was extended, a stone whizzed through the air, and the window so long protected was shattered, and fell into a thousand pieces. A yell of triumph burst from a hundred throats, and every eye was turned upon the hero. He was a great, lank, awkward fellow with a pug-nose, a cold, impertinent eye, thin lips and blinking eyelids, who testified the satisfaction in his achievement simply by a fleeting smile of coarse disdain.

"Is that you, William?" said Bella to him. "Fine occupation for Lord Chatham's son!"

Young William Pitt turned sharply and bent his keen gaze upon the person who had thus apostrophized him. He recognized her and a swift flush stained his pallid cheeks.

"Let me alone," he muttered; "I was only having some fun!" And walking off, he was soon lost in the crowd.

"That boy will never be anything but a ne'er-do-well," said Lady Vereker with a shrug.

Three years later "that boy" became Prime Minister of England, and such a Prime Minister as England had never had before him.

Meanwhile the crowd waxed more turbulent. The ferocity born of pleasure, the longing to destroy, peculiar to such huge assemblies of Englishmen, begin to make themselves manifest.

As there were no more windows to break, what was to be done?

"Pull down the house!" was the cry. "Get a beam and we will set our shoulders to it! Here are twenty good men of like mind! No: fetch some straw and fagots! Set fire to the door! Let us smoke the rats out of their trap!"

A score of figures appeared, ghastly, sinister, suggesting pillage. In the general disorder the libertines grew bolder. The shrieks of women burst from obscure corners, followed by long, brutal laughter.

"I am terrified! I feel as if I were going to faint," gasped Esther.

Although she affected a show of courage, Lady Vereker was beginning to quail.

"Indeed, I did very wrong to come here," she said; "let us try to retrace our steps or gain a side street."

But it was too late. The mob increased with every moment. The crowds of new arrivals pressed down upon them, cutting off the retreat of those who sought to escape the turmoil.

"I am stifling!" cried Esther wildly, as she lost her footing.

At this moment a cry arose:—

"The Guards! the Guards!"

The solid earth trembled beneath the gallop of the troop which had just turned the corner of Pall Mall and were charging up the street. Amidst the frightful tumult there came a second of silence and stupor, during which was heard the ring of hoofs as they struck the pavement and the commands of the officers:—

"Right about! Forward! Draw sabres!"

There was a click of steel and glimmer of blades. An indescribable panic ensued. The people, of late so buoyant, now mad with terror, rushed towards the nearest exit—that is, to some place of safety—with such savage energy and with so formidable an impulse that iron railings were rent before them. Esther felt herself wrenched from Bella so suddenly and with such brutal force that it was a miracle that her arm which encircled Lady Vereker's waist was not left behind her. The human tide hurled her against a house and would have crushed her against the wall had not other human bodies intervened and saved her from the violence of the shock. She found herself at the head of a flight of six stairs without having set foot upon one of them. A large door stood open before her. Twenty persons were projected along with her into the interior in a solid mass, entering the house like an inundation. Esther was saved; the horrible fear which had paralyzed every nerve was relieved, and her heart began to beat again. At the same time, through the open door and high above the desperate cries of those who still struggled in the street, she heard the ringing voice of an officer commanding a halt. The Riot Act was being read, and an occasional fragment of the coldly menacing phrases reached even her ear.

The place into which Esther had been cast was a spacious vestibule, into which surged fresh arrivals without ceasing, despite the efforts of the footmen and of a man who fretted and fumed, and gave useless and inexecutable orders. This man, the proprietor of the place, was Mr. Brooks, and the house was the famous club which bore his name. Poor Mr. Brooks endeavored to confine the crowd to the vestibule, which he was forced to yield to it, as one yields to a conflagration; but already under the pressure of the mass Esther had been thrust into a second antechamber. The air was close and stifling; the situation became critical, while the second danger threatened to become worse than the first.

Suddenly a little door was thrown open, and some one laid hold upon her. In the next instant the door was closed, and the girl found herself in the depths of an arm-chair, where she swooned.

Not entirely, however; she felt in a half-conscious way that some one slapped her hands and blew in her face. A voice murmured, "Some water! Cold water, quick!" Then the person left her, for she felt that she was alone again. Suddenly a great hubbub filled the house. In the street without, now quite deserted, the cavalry swept by like a whirlwind. Then all was silence. With eyes closed, and in a state of semi-consciousness, Esther believed herself alone, when all at once, but a few steps from her, a word was pronounced in an angry tone.

"A doublet!"

Oaths and stifled exclamations accompanied the word. Brought to her senses by curiosity and apprehension, Esther opened her eyes and beheld a remarkable spectacle. It was a vast hall lighted by several lamps suspended from the ceiling. The light, gathered by immense reflectors of tin, fell full upon a long table placed in the centre of the apartment. This table was covered with a green cloth crossed with white lines. Seven or eight men were seated about it, each one having at his side a bowl full of gold pieces and a small tray bearing a cup of tea, a glass, and a flask of brandy. They were engaged in a game of faro.

Nothing could have been more singular than their appearance and attire. Nearly every man wore a large straw hat to screen his eyes from the dazzling light, and perhaps to mask his emotions at the same time; but the most ridiculous part of it was that two or three of the younger gamesters had seen fit to decorate their hats with flowers and ribbons after the fashion of the shepherdesses in the opera. Certain persons, attired with studied refinement, wore leathern cuffs to avoid soiling the lace at their wrists. God save the mark! They would consent to lose a castle in the course of an evening, but would hesitate to spoil a pair of Chantilly ruffles. Others seemed to have lost all respect for themselves. One young man who sat opposite Esther, a sort of good-natured athlete, with big, sensual jaws, and whose tanned face, especially his brow and glance, shone with intelligence and audacity, was so negligent in his attire that his hairy chest appeared beneath his open shirt. Another, an older man, wore his coat turned inside out, through superstitious fancy, as every one was aware; while more than one, with hands concealed beneath the table, feverishly fingered some sort of talisman.

These men appeared to have heard nothing,—neither the cries of the mob, the invasion of the house, the charge of the Guards, nor the entrance of a strange woman into the very room where they were playing. What mattered it all to them? What did it all amount to in comparison with a doublet? As infatuated as Horace's wise man, the end of the world would not have interrupted their game.

Esther felt that her presence was as unperceived as though a charm had rendered her invisible, like the living being whose terrible fate had conducted him on board of the phantom ship. Therefore without a qualm of fear she permitted herself to enjoy the novel scene.

At this moment the banker's *côteau* raked in all the stakes, the rare and fortunate result of drawing two similar cards from his right and left.

"Used up!" exclaimed a stout man with a prodigious sigh, his bowl being empty. In the speaker Esther recognized Stephen Fox, whom she had seen at Drury Lane. His brother, Charles James, the eminent orator, the man with the open shirt, gayly smote his shoulder.

"Shylock will make you a loan," he said; "you have more than a pound of flesh to offer him as security!"

Instead of a laugh, Charley's joke was received with a grunt of approbation.

One man alone seemed insensible to the incidents of the game. This was a gentleman of some sixty years, dressed in accordance with the latest Parisian *mode*. In him Esther recognized George Selwyn, who had been one of the most amiable, one of the wittiest men of his time, but was now absorbed and besotted by a passion more potent than that of gaming.

Up to this time the actress had not seen the banker, whose back was turned to her and who had not uttered a word. At this moment, however, the following disdainful words escaped him: "Ten thousand pounds, and no more! What a shame that I should have played for such low stakes!"

Esther started at sound of that voice, which she had heard not more than twice, but which she recognized instantly. It was Lord Mowbray, that terrible Mowbray, against whose love she had been warned!

A man entered the room and approached her with a glass of water in his hand.

"I see that you are better," he said. "Never mind; drink this to secure your recovery."

Esther hesitated. Still fluttered by the discovery which she had just made, she could not but be mindful of Lady Vereker's warning words. How many times had she read in romances and journals strange narratives of young girls being rendered helpless by narcotics! Ought she to drink, to trust this unknown man? She looked at him, and her perplexity increased. Another enigma to decipher: a generous sentiment pictured upon an evil countenance.

In fact, all the passions seemed to have left their trace upon that worn, pallid, haggard face. His age was uncertain, his condition ambiguous; his accent even sounded a note of doubt upon the nationality of the individual, offering no clew. Was he of middle age or old; valet or gentleman; English or a foreigner? One surprising thing was that the hard, bold manner which might well be habitual vanished before an expression of interest which seemed sincere. As he noted the girl's hesitation a trace of sadness passed over his coarsened features, almost ennobling them.

"I am not thirsty," she said, loath to wound the feelings of one who had already shown her consideration.

And he, regaining his accustomed composure, placed the glass upon a console.

Softly as Esther had spoken, Lord Mowbray had heard her. He turned and bent his stupefied gaze upon her. Esther, alone, in the torn garments of a serving maid, half fainting, in the card-room of the Brooks Club! Assuredly there was food in plenty for his surprise. What fate had sent his prey into his very clutches? Fortune, it is said, never comes single-handed! After the doublet, this fairest flower! And he was just the man to profit by his luck.

"Gentlemen," he said, rising as he spoke, "circumstances oblige me to—"

A cry of indignation interrupted his words, while three or four hands were placed upon his shoulders, forcibly obliging him to resume his seat.

"The game is not over." "We won't permit it!" "Wait until you win another ten thousand!" "This is not fair!"

"So be it!" answered Mowbray with a smile; "only permit me to say one word to Lebeau."

The man who had brought the glass of water approached upon hearing his name, and Lord Mowbray hastily whispered a phrase in a foreign tongue in his ear. Thereupon Lebeau, as we may now call him, returned to the girl.

"The street is free," he said, "but, now that the Guards have passed, the disorder may begin again. If you wish to profit by the lull to make your way home, the minutes are precious. Do you feel strong enough to walk?"

"Yes, certainly."

"Then come."

Esther rose and obeyed him, this time without hesitation. The momentary excitement occasioned by the doublet having subsided, the gamblers had remarked her presence. The glances directed towards her betrayed their curiosity. Despite her disguise, she might be recognized; consequently the necessity of escaping as speedily as possible presented itself. But she did not forget that Lebeau was her guide, the accursed mentor of the greatest libertine in England. The young lord had whispered to his former tutor; evidently the hurried words had reference to her. Therefore she saw the necessity of being upon her guard, ready to fly at the slightest suspicious movement. Meanwhile her heart beat with fear, curiosity and, perhaps, with delight; for it must be admitted that she adored an adventure.

So they went out. The din of the riot came to them from a distance. The street was empty; the night was beautiful and calm. The lights in the lanterns were flickering in their sconces and expiring. The minister's house with its broken windows was guarded by soldiery.

Preceded by a page who carried a torch, Lebeau took the way towards Westminster. It seemed marvellous that he should know so well the location of Miss Woodville's abode.

"Will it please you to give me your arm?" he asked in a slightly changed, humble tone.

She passed her arm within his. Lebeau quickly drew his cocked hat down over his eyes to conceal his glance, and sustained the young girl with an almost tender solicitude, but with discretion and respect.

Thus they walked some distance in silence. At last he began:—

"You distrusted me at first."

She tried to protest, but he added:—

"Oh, you were quite right. Be on your guard. Life is full of snares. I have an intimate acquaintance with my brother man, and I find him bad."

Was he speaking of mankind in general, or of some one in particular? Esther was upon the point of inquiring when they halted in Tothill Street before a low door, upon which Lebeau knocked loudly.

"Some one is coming," he said; "I hear steps in the garden. You have escaped a menacing danger. I do not speak of being crushed beneath the hoofs of the horses; that would be as nothing compared with the other. You are saved, but the peril may threaten you again at any moment. However, it does not signify.

You are in my care."

With these words he turned upon his heel and vanished just as the door was thrown open. Esther found herself confronted by the more severe than anxious face of her cousin Reuben. With his youthful air, his light, fluffy hair and sombre eyes, he resembled one of those avenging angels whom the Lord sent to the guilty cities to pronounce their doom when the hour of repentance had passed and that of retribution had sounded.

"At last!" he muttered in a bitter tone.

"Were you alarmed about me? Has not a man been sent here with a message from Lady Vereker?"

"Yes," answered Reuben with a derisive sneer; "that woman, whose very name is a reproach and a scandal, has had the goodness to assure us that you were in her charge. A strange guardian! Daniel was safer in the lions' den than Esther Woodville under Lady Vereker's wing!"

"You have no idea what has happened? All London is insane over Rodney's victory. They are fighting and breaking windows; the streets are full of soldiers."

"But what means this disguise?"

"I swear to you it was the only means of passing through the crowds."

"I should be glad to believe you," said Reuben, enveloping her in a glance of fire. "Oh, Esther! You who bear the predestined name, the chaste name of the woman who saved the people of God, you who ought to be as pure as the fountain of Gihon, as fresh as the rose of Sharon!"

But Esther abbreviated the biblical effusion.

"I must hasten to relieve my aunt's mind," she said.

"I have advised her to retire without waiting for you."

"That was wise. Good night, Reuben."

"Good night. I am going to pray."

"And I—am going to bed and to sleep."

But she did not sleep as readily as she had anticipated. The events of the day and evening, Sir Joshua's guests, the gamblers at Brooks's with their shepherd hats, the dangers encountered, her new friend Bella, the mysterious personage who had, as it seemed, received orders to plan her ruin, yet had protected her, —all these conflicting subjects created a tumult in her brain.

She cogitated upon the singular destiny which had cast her between the love of a Reuben and that of a Lord Mowbray, between a saint and a demon.

And when at last she sank into the unconsciousness of sleep, between these two personalities, equally imperious and passionate, but actuated by an opposite sentiment, there glided the pale, melancholy visage of Francis Monday.

CHAPTER V.

A STRANGE EDUCATION.

It was late on the following morning ere Lord Mowbray's valet ventured to enter his lordship's chamber. The daylight fell upon the red and swollen eyelids of the sleeper, who opened his eyes and uttered an oath. It was evident that the young nobleman was not in his best humor.

"Is that you, Oliver?"

"Yes, my lord."

"Who is in the antechamber?"

"Your lordship's tailor, who has come to try on the plum-colored coat with the jonquil trimmings; the little glove-woman from Piccadilly, who insists upon a word with your lordship; and Capt. Hackman, who has already called twice to inquire for your lordship."

"Let the tailor wait. Tell the Captain that I shall require his services later, and let him see to it that he brings two fellows of the determined sort along with him. As for the glove-woman, send her away. Because one shows these creatures some little attention of an evening when one is drunk, they think they have rights. Nothing could be more ridiculous, Oliver."

"Assuredly not, my lord."

"Is Lebeau there?"

"Mons. Lebeau has this instant come in."

"Ask him to come to me."

A moment later the former tutor and present factotum of Lord Mowbray smilingly entered the chamber like a man who expects to receive his quietus with a bare bodkin and is disposed to make the best of it.

His lordship addressed him in French.

"*Eh bien*, Lebeau?"

"*Eh bien*, my lord? Did you not receive my message by the little page from Brooks's?"

"Of course I did, and I was furious at such a mischance. Here had fate cast her into my very arms, and your cursed bungling let her escape!"

"Say, rather, the accident of fate, my lord. I was just in the act of putting the little one into a coach, when a band of ruffians, hotly pursued by the soldiers, fell upon us and knocked me down. When I regained my feet, Miss Woodville had vanished, and I was a prisoner in the hands of the guards. In vain I assured them that I was attached to your lordship's service. All that I was able to inform you was that I had failed."

Lord Mowbray looked his confidant full in the eyes.

"You are decidedly growing old," he said.

"That may be."

"Yes, you are growing old, and worse than that. Your compatriots have it that when the devil is old he turns hermit. Are you doing likewise? As God is my judge, Lebeau, I believe you are becoming virtuous."

Lebeau affected an offended air.

"My lord," he retorted, "I believe myself above such a suspicion. My past record answers for me."

"You are joking, but I am serious. Do you know the thought that has suggested itself to me, more especially since yesterday?"

"I cannot fancy, my lord."

"Well, that you are playing me false!"

With folded arms, Lebeau calmly regarded the speaker.

"Playing you false?" he echoed steadily. "For what reason?"

"That is what I wish to know."

"That would be folly on my part. Have you ever known me to commit deliberate treason? Does not my livelihood depend upon you? Are not my pleasures the remnants of yours? Have I not reared you as my own child? If I love anything in this world, it should assuredly be you."

"Then why do you oppose my course with Esther, when she loves me and is ready to yield? I have even feigned to believe you a bungler in order not to believe you a traitor and unfaithful to me. You, who have arranged all my intrigues—why do you oppose this one?"

"I have told you that the affair is full of peril."

"On account of the cousin Reuben?"

"Precisely."

"A psalm-singing hypocrite!"

"You do not know him. The man has a will of iron, and he loves Esther. In a different epoch he would have been capable of subverting a monarchy, and he would set London on fire if his passion, which he regards as sent from on high, should command him to do it. Young as he is, there are hundreds of fanatics who follow and obey him, and I advise Capt. Hackman and his men not to try issues with that legion of fools!"

"You quite fire me to carry the adventure to the issue at all events."

"Then may the devil protect your lordship! As for myself, I have sermonized quite enough for a man of my stamp. In any case, my lord, the receipts of last night's game must have recompensed you for the miscalculations of love. In that regard we have another proverb in our language. When I left the club Fortune seemed to be smiling upon you."

"Yes, and I continued to win until daybreak. Poor Charles Fox hadn't a guinea to his name. Moreover, he was hopelessly intoxicated, and, to cap the climax, had an important speech to deliver to-day. We bound up his head in cold cloths and left him in a chair as well as could be expected. I scrupled about ruining him, for it is said that his furniture will be seized next week; but he does not seem to mind. I won twenty thousand pounds and remained alone with Lord Stavondale. It was raining, and we watched the day dawn across the wet windows. I assure you it is a very ugly sight to see. Stavondale pointed out two drops of water of about equal density slowly coursing over the pane. 'I will wager,' he said, 'that *that* one will touch the sash first.' 'I'll take you,' said I. 'How much?' said he. 'My night's winnings,' said I. Just at that moment a devilish drop, which some inequality in the glass turned from its course, joined Stavondale's drop, which came in with a rush, and I lost my twenty thousand pounds. What consoled me for my loss was the novelty of the invention. This racing drops across a window pane is every whit as amusing as pitting horses against each other at Newmarket."

Here chocolate was brought in at the same time with his lordship's journals.

"See if there is anything in the papers," he commanded.

Lebeau glanced through the *Morning Chronicle* and the *Gentleman's Magazine*, and several other gazettes of the same description, which included magazines both matrimonial and sentimental.

"Let us see," said he; "'In a certain house in the neighborhood of the Thames —' Your lordship knows that this has reference to the House of Commons."

"Pass over politics."

"Here is a book announced from the pen of Mr. Bryant, the antiquarian, who is so well informed concerning events from the origin of the world to the Deluge. Fancy considering nothing of importance *after* the Deluge! His work is disposed of in three words,—'Heavy, tiresome, pedantic.' Cumberland's romance is also treated in three words,—'Refined, sensible, and tender.'"

"Pass over literature."

"The condemned of the week: 'Sarah Hoggs, to be hanged for stealing a piece of cloth that was spread out to dry; Laurence Williamson, to the same penalty for having cut down sundry young trees; item, Annie Smith, to one year's imprisonment for having taken forty shillings in the presence of witnesses;

item, Florence Dunk, to be hanged for having taken five shillings privately; item, William Morton, to transportation for having assassinated his father.'"

"Pass over all that. What society news is there?"

"'Major T—— has again been detected in cheating at cards; he has been requested not to appear at Almack's again.'"

"That's Topham, the editor of the *World*!" exclaimed his lordship. "Bah! in a week's time he will be back again and everybody will be shaking hands with him."

"'Lady B—— has eloped with her husband's groom; his lordship will be consoled by the society of Mlle. Annette, the little French dancer.'"

"Is there nothing else?"

"Nothing but two duels, three abductions, five or six bankruptcies, several fires, and a charade in verse.—Ah!"

"Well, what is it?"

"George Barrington, the gentleman-sharper, has been arrested at Edinburgh!"

"Barrington! a charming fellow! I recollect one evening at Ranelagh, when he showed me how he purloined a snuff-box, and as payment for the lesson he took my watch. And here he is under lock and key! Poor boy!"

"You need not pity him. He will plead his cause so eloquently that he will be acquitted, as he has been many a time."

"In truth, he is a very Cicero among thieves. And the advertisements?"

"The alchemist Woulfe announces for sale an elixir which is a panacea for every malady. Samuel Wollmer will loan money to sons-of-family in embarrassment. As he is actuated by pure love of humanity, his terms will be very moderate. Mrs. Cresswell offers false hair, masks, and red pomade for the lips. Oh, oh! here's a gentleman of middle age who desires to meet a young lady of good appearance and amiable disposition, but discreet and lively. He'll find her," added Lebeau gravely. "I am convinced that his advertisement will be answered."

During this time Oliver had dressed and prepared his master, and had tried on the plum-colored coat with the jonquil trimmings. Every trace of the night's fatigue had disappeared; the fresh hue of early youth bloomed again upon Lord Mowbray's cheek. As he was about to go out he gave his final orders to Oliver.

"You will buy for me 'The Tests of Character'; also, you will ask for the fashionable romance, 'The Cadenas.' You will inquire about the new wax which has just been invented by the Prince of Wales; they say it is marvellous. Now let us go and have a game of bowls, after which we will take a turn in the fencing-school."

Lord Mowbray slipped his arm into that of Lebeau, and in this attitude they went out together, which seemed to announce the return of confidence and friendly feeling. Mons. Lebeau was an adept in the art of pleasing, and in order to make good his return to grace he employed all the resources of his wit, which was by no means of mediocre quality. A curious fellow was this same Lebeau, who had almost ceased to be a Frenchman without wholly becoming an Englishman. He had distinguished himself among the tutors who were furnished to lordlings and who were termed "bear-keepers." He was clever, knew the world, was "up" in literature, could recite from the poets, and in case of need was able to turn a verse as easily as one twirled a snuff-box. He had had a tragedy produced and hissed off the stage somewhere, for he had tasted the cup of a man of letters, living by dedications to the great and by writing homilies for churchmen, rich in skekels but poor in intellect. He would frequently say, "Had I delivered all the sermons which I have written, I should be a cardinal." In turn, doctor upon a vessel of the East India Company, actor, professor of mathematics, courier to an ambassador, Parisian correspondent to a German prince who boasted thirty-three subjects, what callings had he not fulfilled? By what sallies had he not attempted fortune? His life resembled one of those old-fashioned romances, filled, as it was, with adventures which we should consider impossible. An event upon which he never cared to enlarge—some sort of an irregular duel with a personage of dignity—had obliged him to leave his native land. In a London brothel he had made the acquaintance of the late Lord Mowbray, who had taken him into his service on condition that he would procure him something new in the way of emotion. "I am bored to death," explained his lordship; "amuse me. I have used up every resource and am used up myself; invent some plan to revive me. Bear in mind your ability as an author and make my life a poem of delights, an unedited romance. Instead of committing your fancies to paper, realize them with my guineas and for my benefit. To begin with, there is my villa, my 'Folly,' which is being built at Chelsea. Give your orders: the mason, the painter, the upholsterer will obey you." Lebeau accepted the engagement and acquitted himself to the perfect satisfaction of his new patron.

It was he who first invented those marvellous traps by means of which the table disappeared after the first course and came up again laid with a fresh service, which relieved the guests of the espionage of the attendants. It was he, again, who devised, or revived from ancient usage, the perfumed rain, the hail of roses; who offered to his master's friends a *fête* such as Cleopatra gave, a Trimalcion supper and a Borgian night festival; who realized for enchanted senses a corner of the Orient, a dream of the Thousand and One Nights, while the snowflakes fell and the wintry wind outside swept over the denuded country. And Lord Mowbray had the satisfaction of saying to those who congratulated him, "This is a mere nothing."

His friends in their jealousy often said to him, "Lebeau is robbing you." Whereupon he would shrug his shoulders and reply, "How can you expect such a clever fellow not to be a little bit of a swindler?"

Let us give an example of one of his surprising devices. As Lord Mowbray was strolling one evening along the Cheyne Walk by the water he was suddenly seized by three or four ruffians, stripped of his clothing, bound, gagged, and finally thrown into the river. There he gave all up for lost, and, believing himself at death's door, fainted away. He recovered, to find himself at the bottom of a gigantic pie, whence he emerged, to the profound astonishment of a dozen or more of his friends who had assembled for supper.

"What do you think of that for a new sensation, my lord?" inquired Lebeau modestly.

"You own no equal!" exclaimed Mowbray enthusiastically. "I would not part with you for ten thousand pounds!"

But Lebeau inspired contrary sentiments in poor Lady Mowbray, who saw in him her husband's evil genius. When he was about she lost all hope of reclaiming her faithless spouse. A slow fever having succeeded the birth of her only son, she made no effort to live. Why should she? Her son would be enticed from her, as her husband had been. The child, as by some inconceivable hereditary repugnance, avoided her, fled her caresses. She herself, to her deep mortification, never experienced that mysterious and potent attachment which eternally binds the existence of mother and child; and it was under these cruel conditions of life that Lady Mowbray, overwhelmed with misery, weary of suffering, and longing for rest, sank into the arms of death.

She expired unpitied, conjugal love in the higher ranks of society being regarded as a ridiculous anomaly. However, the cynical joy of Lord Mowbray, even in that epoch of irony and indifference, caused a shudder among the less delicate. Henceforth he was in no way hampered. A career of untrammelled debauchery lay open before him; but an unexpected event arrested him with ruthless abruptness. He suddenly disappeared, and the circumstances of his taking-off, at once ignoble and sinister, finally became known in the social walks where he had been best known. He had lost his life in attempting to experiment upon himself in the mysterious sensations which, he was informed, attended the final convulsions of those doomed to die by hanging. Whether through mismanagement or crime, the cord had not been cut in time, and Death still guarded his secret from the one who had essayed to violate it.

Among the deceased nobleman's papers were found sundry instructions for the education of his son, among which one doctrine, far worse than atheism, was drawn up in cold, dry, incisive terms, to suit the custom of the time.

"Man," it maintained, "should live in accordance with nature. Now, nature commands us to flee pain and seek pleasure. Certain philosophers of antiquity have clearly perceived this truth, and that, too, at an epoch when the human mind was not yet encumbered and obscured by vain prejudices. But they have not ventured to demonstrate their theory even unto the end; they have imagined a substance called the soul, the tendencies of which are at constant variance with those of the body. They have arrayed pleasure in the guise of virtue, and have thus opened the way for the Christian folly. Christianity is the most formidable opponent of happiness, and during long ages has rendered the world well-nigh uninhabitable. From infancy we are imbued with the mawkish doctrines; I, myself, have had the utmost difficulty in relieving myself of the yoke and I have but imperfectly succeeded. That is why, should I die before my son has attained his majority, I expressly desire that he shall grow up without receiving the teachings of any religion whatsoever. Later he will understand these aberrations when he comes to a full appreciation of the long series of human errors. Let his mind be developed, stocked with facts, and ornamented with agreeable reflections; let him be schooled in all that pertains to bodily exercise where strength and address are required. By increasing his vigor, his passions will increase and consequently his relish for life. Let him be instructed not to govern or struggle with himself, but to follow in all things the only instinct which can be his certain guide,—that which attracts man to pleasure. Monsieur Lebeau appears to me a man of the world and the one best fitted to take charge of this education."

The will of the dead man was duly accomplished. The young man was reared in the school of evil and became a curious, experimental subject for his master. The late Lord Mowbray had been a reclaimed fanatic; after his own fashion he preached as do nearly all of his compatriots. Lebeau contented himself with observation, and consigned these observations to a certain manuscript, written in French, which was entitled: "A Treatise on Pleasure; or, A Rational Journal of a Young English Nobleman. To be published one hundred years after my death."

Lebeau remarked many things; among others these:—

"This youth, reared in the very lap of happiness, was not happy. The pleasure which formed his daily lessons seemed to him stale and forced. Over and beyond the delights which were multiplied for him and almost imposed upon him, he dreamed of others to which he could not attain, thereby proving that the true vocation of man is the unattainable, the unreal. He was bred according to nature, that is to say, after the fashion of savages; his joys revolved in the narrow, wretched circle in which the primitive inhabitants of the globe vegetate. Five or six thousand years of civilization have delicately undermined, modelled, and ameliorated this block of confused sensations which we represent. The thousand constraints which man has imposed upon himself, and his privations, voluntary or obligatory, not to mention his griefs, have refined him, perfected his organs of pleasure, increased his faculty of happiness an hundred-fold. Suppress these constraints, these tests, these combats, and you leave him but the swift, bestial joys in which the aborigines, our ancestors, forgot for a moment in the obscurity of their caverns the frightful misery of their existence. Young Mowbray at twenty years of age had run the gamut of fallacious love. He had learned the principles of gallantry and debauchery as one learns Latin; but never having trembled, wept, nor suffered, he was totally ignorant of genuine love."

All at once towards Lebeau, that man of infinite complaisance, he experienced a sense of secret resistance. It was upon the day when first he was smitten by the charms of Miss Woodville. A will seemed to interpose between him and the object of his desire, seeming to say: "All women, but not *this one!*"

Was it not sufficient that she had become dearer to him than all others?

CHAPTER VI.

THE HOUSE IN TOTHILL FIELDS.

In her turn Esther had been awakened, as she was every morning, by a sort of dull buzzing, which for a space continued and finally died away. It was Reuben droning the morning prayers in the lower hall in presence of his mother and the aged servant, Maud. She raised herself upon her elbow and glanced about her with an expression of disgust. However, there was nothing displeasing to the sight about the chamber. To be sure, the appointments were of the simplest description, and the walls were bare; but everything exhaled the perfection of neatness and propriety. The window opened upon extensive meadows, called Tothill Fields, where some years later rose the quarter known as Pimlico. On this side no building intercepted the light of day; consequently the fresh, pure radiance of morning flooded the room, flecking the draperies and white furniture. But Esther for a long time had indulged herself in a dream of luxury and grandeur. It seemed to her that each night renewed for her special benefit the story of Cinderella. During the entire evening she walked in her glory beneath the fire of glances, like a little queen, envied, admired, adored, tasting, as an homage more enduring than the applause of men, the jealousy of her comrades. The curtain having fallen, the beautiful costume replaced by a modest gown of some dark stuff, she escaped from the scene of her triumph with her arm firmly locked in that of Mrs. Marsham. When she awoke in the morning there was nothing to prevent her from believing that it had all been a dream, and that she was after all only an ordinary little being destined to set a good example to her neighbors, and be the joy of some commonplace, honest husband. What was there in store for her but to share this insipid existence, take her part in the usual housework, and listen to the babble of her aunt, who represented simple, tender devotion, as Reuben was the exponent of the suspicious and fierce kind? But patience! It would not be long ere emancipation would lend her wings to escape from this irksome prison.

More than ever this morning was she disposed to view her surroundings with a disapproving and dissatisfied eye. When should she have a boudoir like Lady Vereker's, and a gilded coach, a footman with a plumed hat, a great nobleman for her husband, subject to her caprices, sighing at her feet, and breathing soft nothings in the pretty, affected language, mingled with French, which the heroes in the fashionable plays made use of? Like Lord Mowbray, she deceived herself on the score of love, but after a different fashion. He saw in it but the satisfaction of the senses; she, the triumph of vanity. To be forever and a day the personage she appeared to be three evenings out of the week, from seven o'clock until ten; to be in reality ingenuous, anxious, coquettish, and impassioned; to play the comedy, and play it to the life, amidst men who were by no means acting; to heave real sighs, shed genuine tears, commit actual follies,—such was her idea of happiness, which would have been perverse had it not been childish.

Scarcely was she dressed ere she received a tender missive from Lady Vereker which informed her of the result of their evening's frolic. One of her ladyship's cousins, an officer in the Guards, had rescued her from her dilemma. For hours she had sought her companion; then she had gone home, "heaping reproaches upon herself and calling herself every manner of barbarous name." For she felt in her heart that "she should never taste of perfect bliss if separated from her incomparable friend, and that it would be inhuman long to deprive her of her presence." This jargon, which passed in the fashionable world of that day, was new to Esther, and she replied in a similar vein, assuring her noble protectress that, had she listened to the dictates of her heart, she would have flown to her: but circumstances obliged her to defer the joy for which she sighed so ardently; the circumstances being a guitar lesson, a new *rôle* to study, and a second sitting with Sir Joshua.

In fact, the guitar master, Mr. O'Flannigan, shortly made his appearance upon horseback, the animal being as lean and lanky as himself. He was an Irish gentleman, descended from the kings of his native land. He was wont to prate of vast domains which had fallen two centuries before his birth into the hands of the English. Thanks to the revolt of the American colonies, which Ireland was preparing to imitate, Mr. O'Flannigan had hopes of regaining his family rights and possessions. Meanwhile he rambled about London, darned his own stockings, and gave music lessons. Moreover, he occasionally relieved old Hopkins, the prompter at Drury Lane Theatre; but whatever he did, he did with innate nobility and elegance. He could bow with a grace almost equal to that of any Frenchman, having passed one week of his youth in Paris, "the capital of elegance and good taste."

It was averred that, like the majority of his countrymen, he must have kissed the famous Blarney stone which communicates to the lips which have pressed it the gift of suave falsehood. But the persons who spoke in that way were his enemies. And who has not an enemy? Mr. O'Flannigan possessed his share of those troublesome individuals, although he had obliged at least three of them to bite the dust.

"What! Three men stretched upon the ground? Three men killed by you single-handed?"

"All of that, miss!"

His brow clouded at the recollection; he declined to enlarge upon the subject; whereupon, since no one wished to wound his feelings by insisting upon details, he would recount the entire dreadful tale even unto the bitter end. One was an Italian, of the princely house of Castellamare; he understood the secret thrust, you know,—the famous secret thrust! Poor man! His death had served no great purpose. To-day the violets bloom upon his grave. Another was a German baron,—a boor who, in passing Mr. O'Flannigan, had knocked over his glass of milk with the tip of his sword and had not known enough to beg his pardon,—a man so tall and stout that he could not have passed through yonder door; yet this Colossus had fallen before little O'Flannigan!

"But why renew these cruel memories? It is a frightful thing for a sensible, philosophic man thus to give the *coup de grâce* to a fellow-man! Now, then, Miss Woodville, if you please. One—two—we are in the key of *fa*."

One day Mrs. Marsham found O'Flannigan in the midst of explaining to his pupil the principles of his favorite art. With her left hand upon her hip, her body proudly curved, her cheeks aglow, and her eyes dancing with pleasure, Esther attacked and parried imaginary thrusts, while she poked with a long cane the bony old body of O'Flannigan, who applauded rapturously, though he rubbed his sides.

"Are you mad, monsieur?" she cried. "Giving fencing lessons to my niece!"

"Madame, I am the humblest of your servants!"

O'Flannigan performed the sword salute with the cane he held in his hand, and attempted to deposit a kiss upon the mitten of the Quakeress, who found herself quite disarmed in spite of herself by such a display of courtesy and high breeding.

"Come, come, Monsieur O'Flannigan," she breathed; "suppose you return to your music."

"At your command, madame.—Now, then, mademoiselle; one—two—three. We are in the key of *sol*!"

After the Irishman's departure, Esther passed the remainder of the morning in walking up and down the little garden, studying the charming *rôle* of Beatrice in "Much Ado about Nothing," which she was to play in a few days. Then came the dinner hour, which reunited Mrs. Marsham, her son Reuben, Esther, and the ancient Maud; since, in accordance with the usage of the sect, the servants consorted with their masters and sat at table with them. Moreover, Maud was no ordinary servant. She possessed the sense of second sight. At certain hours she prophesied and spoke in a strange tongue which no one understood. "The Spirit is upon her!" they were wont to say respectfully upon such occasions. Very deaf and purblind, even with her double vision Maud could not see the spiders' webs which festooned the ceiling; she could hear "voices," though not that of her mistress when it called her. Any one in the wide world except the Marshams would have quickly recognized the inconvenience of having a vaticinal cook.

At the dinner-table the dangers which Esther had encountered upon the preceding night became the topic of conversation. Mother and son regarded the event from their own standpoints. The former blessed Providence who had guided the girl through her peril safe and sound; the latter cursed the malice of the men who had madly risked their lives in breaking a minister's windows for the glorification of a stupid soldier. How many there were who would have permitted themselves to be killed for Rodney, who would not have raised a finger for Christ! Esther uttered not a word concerning Lord Mowbray; she simply spoke of the excellent gentleman who had escorted her home.

"The brave man!" said Mrs. Marsham. "I long to know and thank him."

"I saw him leaving, or rather flying, like a malefactor," muttered Reuben. "Would he not have remained to receive our thanks, if he had thought he deserved them?"

"Virtue is diffident, my son; her right hand knoweth not what her left hand doeth."

Reuben only replied by an imperceptible shrug of his shoulders. The repast over, Maud returned to her kitchen, where she held forth all alone for several long hours. Mrs. Marsham installed herself in her rush-seated chair and adjusted a pair of silver-and-horn spectacles upon the tip of her nose, the rigid steel mounting of which suggested the curved arch of some ancient bridge. She selected one of her favorite books, the "Pilgrim's Progress," or the life of George Fox, which for thirty years had fascinated her timid, childish imagination. Soon the regular breathing, like the purring of a great drowsy cat, informed Esther that her aunt was in Morpheus's arms. Indeed, she had fallen asleep with an ecstatic smile upon her features. Perhaps she dreamed that she walked in a fair garden, attended by angels, and that one came to her, clothed in white raiment, with a lily in his right hand, and said to her, "Good morrow, my good Mrs. Marsham. How are you? My father will be rejoiced to see you." And then, stooping, he would gather stars from the *parterre* of heaven and arrange them in a bouquet for the elect; for Mrs. Marsham was frequently favored with such dreams, and upon awakening she would recount them to her friends as did the personages in the Old Testament. She was forever searching some explanation of them, since she considered them in the light of celestial visions.

"She sleeps, and is happy," said Reuben in a lowered tone. "Would that I could find repose!"

"Why can you not?" asked Esther negligently.

"Because my heart is troubled by the thought of the iniquities which are committed in Israel. Sometimes it seems to me that I am a scapegoat, and that all the sins of England are upon me."

"Rather a heavy burden, my poor cousin!"

"Oh, do not laugh, Esther; for it is you who are to be pitied; it is for you that I weep."

"For me?"

"Yes, for you, and because of your fatal beauty."

"Fatal! I take the compliment from whence it comes, and am charmed to know that you consider me even passing fair. But pray tell me why my beauty is fatal."

"Listen and give heed, Esther. You have read the Holy Scriptures?"

"Yes."

"When God imprints upon the face and body of woman a charm which renders the wisest fools, there is a hidden reason which should be visible if we would but open our eyes. He has created her for the salvation or the perdition of a variety of men. Eve worked the ruin of Adam; Bethsheba unconsciously corrupted the holy king; Delilah delivered Samson over to his enemies; Salome snatched from Herod's luxury the condemnation of the Precursor. On the contrary, Ruth exhaled joy and consolation about her; Esther softened the anger of a terrible king and saved the people of God; Jabel drove a nail into the temple of Sisera; Judith delivered Bethulia by cutting off the head of Holofernes. Which will you be, a Delilah or a Judith?"

"Neither, I hope. In the first place, pray do not count upon me to cut off anybody's head. I am a sorry coward, and I have a horror of seeing blood. The other day I saw a dog with a bleeding paw, and I thought I should faint."

"Ah!" exclaimed Reuben bitterly, "better were it to cause the impious to lose every drop of blood in his veins than to inspire a single evil thought in the just. I feel within myself that it is a sin to look upon you; my will totters when for too long a space my eyes have rested upon those shoulders, that slender form, those brilliant eyes, that bud-like mouth. Sometimes it seems to me that I would suffer eternal damnation for you, and that I should find an abominable pleasure in it! How many times have I prayed God to destroy those adorable features which it has pleased him to create! Willingly would I obliterate and annihilate them!"

"Are you going mad?" cried Esther in alarm. "And yet you say you love me!"

"Yes," replied Reuben: "we alone know how to love, because we alone know how to hate,—we, the sons of the saints whose hearts are full of bitterness and sorrow. They do not love who live in joy and pleasure. My love increases with the tears that it causes me to shed, with the combats that I undergo for you, and, moreover, with the fury that I experience against those who raise their eyes upon your beauty!"

Involuntarily he had raised his voice. The old lady awoke with a start.

"Naughty children!" she murmured querulously. "Quarrelling again?—you who were born to understand one another, and to be happy!"

CHAPTER VII.

CONFIDENCES.

Esther succeeded in persuading good Mrs. Marsham that she ought not to accompany her to her next sitting with Sir Joshua, since the great painter desired to be alone with his model. The age and eminent reputation of the President of the Academy removed far from him all suspicion; consequently there was nothing to be done but to respect his wishes. Therefore Esther went alone to Leicester Fields in a sedan-chair borne by a couple of doughty Irishmen; but she could not repress a movement of impatience upon perceiving Reuben on horseback following her at a short distance with his sombre glance. When she entered the house the young man quickly alighted, attached the bridle of his horse to the railing of the square, and, seating himself upon a bench, fixed his eyes upon Sir Joshua's door.

"Shadowed!" murmured the girl.

The desire of deceiving one's jailers, the omnipresent dream of evasion which ever haunts the prisoner, filled her mind and inclined her to anger.

"Bah!" she thought, "my deliverance is close at hand."

She swiftly mounted the stairs which led to the studio, and was received by Francis Monday.

"The President has been unexpectedly summoned to an audience with his Majesty, who has come in from Kew to St. James's this morning," he explained. "Be so good as to wait for Sir Joshua, who will return before long. Shall I request Miss Reynolds to come and keep you company?"

"Why disturb her? There are so many curious things here to amuse one! One might pass a whole day looking about this apartment without being bored for a moment."

"So be it!" replied Frank in a slightly tremulous voice. "Shall we look about together?"

He forthwith proceeded to show her all the rare objects arranged in order within their glazed cases, giving her explanations of everything. There were snuff-boxes, fans of which one was said to be the work of the poet Pope, and foreign arms brought home by Sir Joshua from a journey in barbaric lands. Frank also named the originals of the unfinished portraits which awaited upon their easels the good pleasure of the painter.

The door of the adjoining apartment, whence the girl had seen him emerge upon the preceding day, stood ajar; she quickly glanced within and saw a quantity of antique casts spread upon large tables, and plaster heads heaped one upon another.

"It is there that I paint," he said, "in order that I may always be near at hand in case Sir Joshua should call me."

"As yesterday," she said rashly; then, realizing the memory which she had evoked, she blushed. As for him, he became pale. However, she soon continued:—

"Sir Joshua loves you very dearly."

"He treats me with an almost paternal kindness; I respect him, and entertain for him the affection of a son. I owe him all that—"

"Yes, I know."

"Ah, but you cannot know all. Perhaps you have been told that I have been adopted and educated by Sir Joshua, but if you only knew from what a future of misery and despair he has snatched me, from what a hell he has saved me!"

He pronounced these words with so simple, so profound an accent that the girl, suddenly touched with sympathy, bent her eyes upon him and said:—

"Where were you before you knew him, and what did you do?"

"I lived with the pirates of the Thames, who forced me to learn their horrible business."

"But how happened it that you fell into such hands?"

"I know not. I know neither my birthplace nor my parents. Even my true age is unknown to me. I have nothing in the world, not even so much as a name— only a surname; they called me Mishap. Perhaps my parents were like those wretches. The thought has often come to me, and driven me almost desperate."

Esther did not speak, but her eyes assured Frank that she was listening with deepest interest.

"We lived in a hovel," he continued, "down by the water, opposite Greenwich, and sometimes in a half-decayed barge on the river which was anchored some twenty yards from shore. By day they sent me on land to beg, and beat me if I returned empty-handed. At low tide I used to search the mud which the sea left dry when it retired."

"For what purpose?"

"To look for things which might have fallen into the water. One found all sorts of stuff on the bed of the river,—wood, rope, bits of cloth, and rusty iron. Frequently I encountered fearful things there, such as human remains, bodies of the unfortunate whose death had been unknown and would never be avenged."

"Heavens! what a dreadful business!"

"You are right: a dreadful business indeed! Those who carry it on are called mud-larks; yet little do they resemble those tiny voyagers of the air which sing so proudly, so joyously, which build their nests in the furrows and soar aloft to heaven's gate. The mud-larks crawl along their wretched way, sometimes immersed to the knees in the icy slime, and frequently they fall victims to the fever as the result of their long searches. Nevertheless, the Thames has engulfed much riches, and sometimes it gives it back. There have been cases of poor wretches finding precious jewels there. One summer's day, during a season of excessive drought, the tide being lower than usual, I espied something glittering in the rays of the rising sun. I stooped; it was an old gold piece bearing the effigy of Charles II. Perhaps for a century it had slept there in the mud."

After a moment of silence he continued:—

"How carefully I wiped it! How I caressed it! How long I contemplated that little coin! At first I decided that I would show my treasure-trove to no one. But where could I hide it? I wore neither shoes, stockings, nor shirt; nothing but an old ragged jacket and trousers without pockets. When I was permitted to go to bed I slept upon a sack filled with rags, along with a boy older than myself. I passed the coin from one hand to the other; I even put it in my mouth beneath my tongue. It seemed a fortune in my eyes, and I thought that when I went to London I should be able to buy out the whole town. Yes; ah, but I was way-wise for my years, and I foresaw what would take place were I to offer my sovereign for sale as the gentlemen did. The dealer would exclaim, 'Such as you with a gold piece! You have stolen it!' Forthwith I should be sent to prison, and from there to the smoky hall of the Old Bailey, where I had seen many a little thief condemned to twenty or thirty lashes. I saw myself bound to the terrible wooden bench, black with human blood; I saw the executioner approach with his awful cat-o'-nine-tails. My thin knees knocked together as I drew the mental picture."

"And what did you do?"

"I determined to hide my sovereign under a tuft of grass on the river bank near Deptford. And I went there often to take a peep at it, while I waited for better days. Alas! there came a great tempest in September; the river rose and overflowed its banks; my hiding-place, my treasure, all disappeared!"

"Poor boy!"

"All these miseries were as nothing compared with others. The worst work was that which I was made to do at night. Of foggy evenings our boat slipped along like a phantom, with the oars muffled in bits of old wool so that they moved without a sound. Thus we circled about the big ships at anchor, or prowled around the sleeping warehouses. At such hours the river belonged to the bandits, to the vagabonds who were called light-horsemen; they were alone, and sovereign masters there."

"But what part did you play upon these nocturnal expeditions?"

"They made me climb up a knotted rope to the bowsprits of the ships, which they knew to be but poorly guarded by the drunken sailors at that time of night. From there I would crawl to the deck. Then I would glide into the storeroom and bring thence a bag of 'sand,' a sack of 'peas,' or a bottle of 'vinegar,' which is pirate slang for sugar, coffee, and rum. When I had lowered my booty into the boat moored under the bow, I would let myself down, my teeth chattering, half dead with fright."

"Were you aware that you were doing wrong?"

"No: no one had taught me the difference between good and bad; no one had ever pronounced in my presence the name of God, unless it was with the accompaniment of some frightful blasphemy. I was simply aware that there existed another race of men who waged war upon my masters; that when the landsmen captured our water-folk they dragged them into a great black house called Newgate, and from there to a place called Tyburn, where they set up a gallows. I saw many of my companions hanged there, for thieves never miss an execution. Have you ever seen a hanging, Miss Woodville?"

"Oh, never!" cried Esther shudderingly.

"You would think it a festival. All along Holborn stagings are set up for those who wish to see, and tables for the wine-bibbers. The mob laughs and sings, and jokes the ladies who have hired windows, and who hide their faces behind their fans. Venders of apples and gin thrust their handcarts into the thick of the crowd. The mountebanks perform their tricks and dances as at the fair of Saint Bartholomew, while the street urchins for half a penny proclaim the complaint against the doomed man. At last he appears upon a cart drawn by a wretched hack, which itself seems on its way to slaughter. I have seen certain men in this plight who were bold and impudent in the face of death, who winked at the women, and responded to the jeers of the crowd. Yes, I have heard them try to sing songs, which the mob took up in chorus. But there have been others!—those who were deaf to everything, deaf even to the exhorting voice of the clergyman. Quivering like dead animals with every jolt of the cart, fainting, convulsed, livid, horrible to look upon, their eyes dilated with terror, they seemed scarcely human, scarcely living but for the evidence of their fear."

He paused for an instant, paling at the recollection. "I saw it all," he pursued, "and knew that after twenty or thirty years of infamy that fate would be mine. If I refused to obey my masters a few blows of the gasket very soon got the better of my resistance. To be beaten by the mud-larks or lashed by the hangman—such was the frightful choice which was offered me, such the view of life which I enjoyed for eight years. Eight years! The age of dependence, confidence, and joy! The age which should know the sweetness of a mother's love and caress!"

Esther's eyes filled with tears as she grasped poor Frank's hands and held them in her clasp.

"Neither have I known a mother," she said; "but I have not suffered as you have. Those about me were kind enough, and I can smile when I compare my miseries with yours."

"One night," continued Frank, "when I refused to play my part in an expedition with the pirates, one of them in a fit of rage threw me into the dark river which hissingly closed over my head."

Esther uttered a cry as though she saw it all, saw with her own eyes the child plunge headlong into the water.

"Fortunately I could swim. I knew the river and it seemed less wicked, less hostile than man. It almost seemed like a mother to me, since it had rocked me upon its bosom and nourished me for so many years. I succeeded in gaining the shore, where I wandered about, shivering, until daybreak. I don't see what prevented my dying, except that such wretches as I are blessed with more enduring vitality than others. Nevertheless, I had some terrible trials to bear. For several days I subsisted upon mouldy crusts floating in the water, cabbage leaves, and other rubbish which I picked up about the market-places. I devoured these sad repasts while inhaling the odor of roasts in Cheapside and Fleet Street. Now and again a charitable gentleman would give me alms without my daring to solicit it other than with my wretched, famished glances. At night I slept sometimes in a church porch, sometimes in an abandoned stable, sometimes under an old wall, which screened me from the wind. One morning I lay asleep, with a stone for a pillow, in the neighborhood of Covent Garden, when I was awakened by a strange voice which seemed to address me. I saw a middle-aged gentleman of modest appearance, with a kind and venerable air, who stood gazing upon me as he leaned on his silver-headed cane. This cane and his old-fashioned wig would have caused me to divine that he was a doctor, had I known the costumes of the different professions.

"'My boy,' he said to me, 'what are you doing there? Why are you not at home at such an hour? Surely your parents must be anxious about you.'

"I answered him rudely, for I knew no other mode of speech.

"'I have no home, and no parents.'

"'What is your name?'

"'They call me Mishap.'

"'Well, friend Mishap, I am going to give the lie to your name, for I am going to take you to the best man in the world.'

"I rose and followed him. Later I learned that he was Levet, the French surgeon of the poor, so poor himself that Dr. Johnson had given him an abiding-place in his house. Thither he led me. The doctor, too, in his time had suffered from poverty and hunger. In his old age he returned good for the evil which he had suffered in his youth. His home was, and still is, a sort of asylum and hospital. With Levet lived Mrs. Williams, the blind poetess, and the negro Frank, whom the author of 'Rasselas' treated more as a friend than a servant. These good people gave me a cordial greeting. They gave me breakfast and made me tell them my story. For the first time in my life I ate of white bread and listened to decent language. Then my heart, which lay like a stone in my breast, melted, and I wept hot tears. They baptized me next day, the good negro being my humble godfather. To the Christian name of Francis they added, for want of a family name, the name of the day on which I had been discovered shivering in my sleep. Some days later, well washed and newly clothed, with shoes and stockings on my feet, all of which seemed strange to me and not a little awkward, I accompanied Dr. Johnson to this house, and in this very room made my first bow to Sir Joshua, who at the time was painting the portrait of Kate Fisher. I can still see the pretty creature, who had brought her friend, Mary Summers, with her. One was all beauty; the other, all wit—component parts of Aspasia.

"'My dear sir,' said the doctor in his grand, solemn way, 'I have brought with me a child for Ugolino to eat.'

"The speech made me shudder, while every one present laughed. Later it was explained to me that during the intervals between his engagements Sir Joshua caused an aged street-paver, who had fallen into necessitous circumstances, but who possessed an expressive head, to sit for him. His name was White, but one day Mr. Burke, seeing him in the lower hall, said to Sir Joshua, 'That man would make an admirable Ugolino.' And from that time he was never called by any other name. It suggested to my master the idea of making him the centre of a great composition representing Dante's terrible scene; but it was necessary to find some children with whom to surround Ugolino. Now you understand the doctor's joke. 'Here is something for you to do,' remarked Sir Joshua to me, 'which will be easier than working for the mud-larks.'

"'What must I do?' I inquired.

"'Remain perfectly quiet, which you may find rather difficult at your age.'

"'It could never be difficult for me to obey and please you,' said I.

"I was given a sort of chamber in the garret, which I still occupy; and from that day I led the life of those by whom I was surrounded. Living from morning till evening amidst painting and designing, the desire to try my hand came to me. I armed myself with a bit of chalk and a slate. Sir Joshua surprised me in the midst of my occupation, and when I made an attempt to conceal my sketch, he remarked: 'Do you know upon what and with what I made my first picture? Upon a scrap of sail-cloth and with a pot of paint which had been left upon the strand at Plympton by the boat-painter.' He looked at my sketch, and the result of his examination was that he sent me to the Royal Academy, which had recently been opened. There I sketched the faces of all the young women who represented Dido or Ariadne. My companions blew peas at them until they made them cry. Then they would clap their hands and pretend that they had given the models the desired expression. I did not know what they meant, but when I had filled my sketch-book to the very last page with Didos and Ariadnes, I respectfully confessed to Sir Joshua that I had much rather paint trees, flowers, grass, and, more than all, water. My dear, great river, where I had lived so long, the ever-changeful home of my infancy!—I am never weary of depicting it, by turns dull as a leaden disk, brilliant as a mirror of burnished steel, now ruffled and agitated, now radiant and peaceful, little rural stream that it is at Hampton Court, arm of the sea at Gravesend, with its perspectives, its shore life, the ships which fleck its surface, and the seafarers it bears upon its bosom."

"Then," inquired Esther, "am I to understand that you are happy?" The young man lowered his eyes and was silent for a moment.

"I am," he answered, "profoundly grateful to my master for all his kindness, for the friendship which every one testifies for me, and for the interest which such men as Mr. Burke and Dr. Johnson take in my studies. But can I be wholly happy? Nothing can replace the affection of a mother,—unless it be that of a wife. There is a void in my heart. Will it ever be filled?"

So humble, so penetrating was the accent of the poor, lonely fellow at this moment that Esther was more deeply moved than she had been by the recital of his boyish sufferings. In her turn her eyes drooped as if, in the young man's words, something had particularly affected her.

"Ah!" he murmured, "you are laughing at me now; but, since I began to speak and you deigned to listen to me, I have told you all. Now I am going to show you the one who, since my entrance into this house, has consoled and sustained me in the hours of discouragement and sadness." And taking her by the hand, he led Esther into his studio, before an unframed picture, from which he drew aside the drapery which covered it.

"A portrait! A portrait of a woman!"

In fact it was the counterfeit presentment of a young woman clothed in white. The picture was still unfinished. The attire, the accessories, the background were scarcely indicated; the head alone seemed almost complete. It was a fine, delicate head, softly illumined by a faint smile as by a ray of autumnal sunshine, the eyes of a dull blue, hesitant in glance as though weary of the light,—infinite weariness in the inclination of the neck and the droop of the shoulders. An indefinable charm of sorrow and resignation overspread the entire countenance. The very uncertainty of the sketch lent to it an ethereal, almost supernatural character, enveloping it in that vague, ideal film which veils the figures in a dream.

"Who is this lady?" inquired Esther.

"She died twenty years ago, and I never saw her in life. I only know that she is called Lady Mowbray."

"Lady Mowbray! The mother of young Lord Mowbray whom you resemble so closely?"

"The same."

"But why has the portrait remained unfinished?"

"The death of the original interrupted the sittings. She knew that she was doomed and wished to bequeath her portrait to her son; but apparently no one cared for her or respected her last wish, since the sketch has never been claimed by the family. It is said that she was most unhappy, and wept her life away. I am as attached to this portrait as to a living person. It watches me and smiles upon me; I speak to it and it responds. How many times have I kissed those poor hands which are now folded in death! I have wished that my mother might resemble her, and in my folly I have more than once addressed her by that holy name. Athwart the space which separates us my heart yearns towards her. What would I not give to have known and consoled her! What do you think of such foolishness, Miss Woodville?"

"I understand you; I assure you that I understand you, and it seems to me that from to-day I shall no longer be the same, that I shall be less frivolous, less thoughtless, that I shall regard life with other eyes."

And turning suddenly she came in contact with an object in the shadow, which upon being disturbed gave forth a queer sound, like to the click of *castagnettes*.

"What is that?" she exclaimed.

"That is nothing, only a skeleton used in anatomical studies."

He drew into the light the singular companion, whose arms and legs projected absurdly every which way. One would have said that it was a drunken sailor attempting a hornpipe. As if to increase its height a lace cap with red ribbons, carelessly placed upon its cranium, had slipped to one side, suggesting the idea of ghostly joviality. Esther burst into a laugh which she quickly repressed.

"Poor thing!" she said. "Like us, he has possessed a heart and a brain. Perhaps he has loved, perhaps they have said he was handsome. Pardon me that I laughed, poor skeleton!"

The words of her well-beloved poet recurred to her memory.

"Do you remember where Hamlet, in the graveyard, holds the jester's skull in his hands? 'Here hung those lips that I have kissed I know not how oft. Where be your gibes now? your gambols? your songs? your flashes of merriment that were wont to set the table on a roar?'"

"'To what base uses we may return, Horatio!'" added Frank.

"Yes," she replied; "'Imperial Cæsar, dead and turn'd to clay, might stop a hole to keep the wind away.'" And she recited the verses which close the scene.

Frank listened with a sort of religious tenderness.

"You love Shakespeare?" he asked.

"I adore him!"

Attracted by this new bond of common admiration, they spoke of that sovereign master of souls, and exchanged the emotions which he had aroused in their hearts. Hand in hand they wandered, and lost themselves in that vast, murmurous forest filled with alarms and enchantments, with refreshing springs and hideous pools, with jocund imps and menacing monsters, where the fairy flowers of sentiment bloom and fade in the umbrage of gigantic thoughts, amidst which passes, like a stormy wind, a tremor of the vague Beyond, the breath of the invisible, unknown world.

As they conversed thus, seated upon an old sofa between the skeleton and the portrait of Lady Mowbray, Reynolds entered. For two hours they had been together. The painter looked at them, and smiled with indulgent penetration.

"We have been talking of Shakespeare," Frank explained, slightly ill at ease.

Sir Joshua did not believe one word of it. Either he knew not, or he had forgotten that old age alone requires to *speak* of love. In youth, love impregnates every word, insinuates itself into the very gestures, plunges into the glance, exhales at every pore, saturates the air we breathe. Then of what import are words?

"And there is Reuben waiting all this while!" thought Esther suddenly.

That thought alone re-established all her roguish coquetry in the space of one second.

CHAPTER VIII.

MR. FISHER'S SUBSTITUTE.

"Mr. Fisher!"

Thus invoked by his name, the hairdresser who had the honor of attending the leading artists of the Theatre Royal, Drury Lane, stopped suddenly upon the dim staircase which led to the dressing-rooms.

"Who is it?" he inquired, striving to distinguish the person who had accosted him. "What do you want? I am in a hurry. Miss Woodville waits. What! *You*, my lord?" he added as his interlocutor advanced into the doubtful radiance shed by the argand-lamp upon the upper landing.

A trifle arrogant at first, with a mingling of poorly dissimulated nervousness (for courage was not Mr. Fisher's besetting virtue), the tone of the worthy hairdresser had become obsequious in the extreme. Lord Mowbray was one of his best clients.

"Mr. Fisher," said the young nobleman, "you are going straight home and to bed."

"I, my lord! Your lordship must surely be jesting. They are waiting for me up-stairs, and I must—"

Lord Mowbray barred his further progress.

"I am not jesting, Mr. Fisher. I can be serious when serious matters are at stake, and there is nothing more serious than the health of an honest man like yourself. I tell you that you have a high fever and that you are going straight to bed, where you will keep warm and let Mrs. Fisher bring you a ptisan."

"But I have no fever, and even if I had I should not fail to perform my duty. And this, a first-night! Why, the king and queen are to honor the performance with their presence!"

"Well, let us cut the matter short, Mr. Fisher. Here is somewhat to sweeten your ptisan."

With the words a handful of guineas changed hands, the jingle of which possessed a persuasive virtue all their own; whereupon the hairdresser began to comprehend that it is sometimes to one's advantage to be feverish.

"But, my lord," he faltered, "would you have Miss Woodville go on the stage with dishevelled hair? Who will take my place?"

"I will, Fisher."

"Can your lordship dress a head of hair?"

"I studied the art in Paris under the celebrated Leonard."

"Is it so!"

"Indeed it is. The man who does not know how to dress a woman's hair misses one of the greatest delights in life. That is why, my dear friend, your art was the most agreeable to Venus; and Mons. Lebeau, my tutor, a man-of-the-world, failed not to give me ample instruction."

"Well, I am flambergasted now!"

"Make haste to pull yourself together and be off, or you will take more cold on this staircase. Quick; hand me the comb, the powder, and the patch-box. Good night, Fisher; take good care of yourself. Devil, man! You'll find you cannot trifle with a fever."

A minute later the false hairdresser, having duly knocked at the door and received permission to enter, walked into a narrow room in which Miss Woodville was dressing, assisted by a maid, under the watchful direction of her aunt, Mrs. Marsham.

"Come, Mr. Fisher," said Esther without looking at the intruder, "we must make haste or I shall be late. Make me just as pretty as you possibly can, for the king will be in the audience."

"I shall do my best, Miss Woodville."

"But this man is not Fisher!" cried the old lady.

Esther cast one swift glance at Mowbray, caught the kerchief about her shoulders, and mechanically plunged her blushing face into the ivory horn which served to protect her eyes and lashes while her hair was being powdered.

The young nobleman respectfully saluted the Quakeress.

"Mr. Fisher is ill," he exclaimed.

"Oh, poor Fisher! What ails him?"

"He has a fever, madam,—a high fever. It would break your heart to hear the poor man's teeth chatter. So I have come in his place."

"It is impossible for you to dress my hair!" gasped Esther.

"Impossible! And why, if you please?" "Because—because—

why, you cannot, you don't know how!"

"I have studied under the best masters. It is not for me to disparage Mr. Fisher; but I venture to say that my touch is more classic than his. I have worked for the French court."

"No, no!" breathed Esther with veiled eyes.

"But, my child," said her aunt in a lowered tone, "you are unreasonable. This boy appears to know his business; besides, he has worked for the French court. Moreover, time presses."

"If Miss Woodville will deign to intrust her head to my care, all will be well," added the would-be hairdresser.

Esther saw there was no help for it but to yield. Suffused with blushes and pouting, though deeply moved, she took her chair before the mirror.

"What style will it please you this evening,—*capricieuse* or *tout amiable*? But I am wrong: a face like yours demands a suitable accompaniment. Esther Woodville—pardon my liberty of speech—should have her hair dressed *à la* Esther Woodville!"

"Anybody can see at a glance that you came from Paris," interposed Mrs. Marsham; "you know how to pay compliments. I fear that your talents may stop there, and that your comb is by no means the equal of your tongue."

"Madam shall be the judge. By his work is the artist known."

With a firm, experienced hand he seized the loosened tresses which overspread the girl's shoulders. Bending above her, inhaling her very personality, he spoke not, he hardly breathed, overcome by the violence of his emotions; while she, bending slightly forward, maintained a strange immobility. A cloud passed before his eyes; his brain reeled. Could he maintain the mastery of himself sufficiently to play the comedy to the end?

All at once a confused turmoil arose from the street below. Mrs. Marsham pricked up her ears.

"Can it be the king already?" she exclaimed.

In order to understand the true import of those two monosyllables, "the king," for the good lady, we must go back a quarter of a century to the time when George III., aged sixteen years, still dwelt in Leicester Fields with his mother, the Dowager Princess of Wales. Never did he pass through Long Acre on his way to the theatre, of which he was a constant patron, without casting a timid glance at pretty Sarah Lightfoot, where she sat at the desk in her father's shop, with her snow-white gown, her folded kerchief, and her glossy tresses innocent of powder. The young Quakeress would bend her head with a light blush beneath the mute and tender contemplation of those big, guileless eyes, undoubtedly more eloquent than their owner had any idea they were. The royal child would pause for a moment, and, heaving a sigh, would continue his way with his unequal, halting gait.

Long, long ago had his Majesty forgotten Sarah Lightfoot; but Sarah Lightfoot, the present Mrs. Marsham, had never forgotten his Majesty. Athwart her dull, peaceful, uneventful existence the charming memory cast a ray which but increased in brilliancy as the days wore on. She had never mentioned the subject in the presence of her son, fearing the disdainful shrug of Reuben's shoulders, and suspecting that he nourished some vague republican chimera; but she would speak complacently with her niece of the king's fancy, save that she asked God's pardon for indulging in such frivolous thoughts.

This was the reason why, on this particular evening, she had scarcely noticed Mr. Fisher's substitute, and why she was so attentive to the sounds in the street. She intended to see the king's arrival, for it seemed to her that the ovation intended for his Majesty by his loyal subjects in some remote way touched her. Mowbray knew nothing of these circumstances, but he confusedly divined that by means of the good woman's curiosity he might rid himself of her presence.

"The king?" said he. "Of course it is he; if you wish to see him you have no time to lose."

For one moment Esther thought to detain her aunt, but how could she explain her perturbation without admitting the whole deceit, without causing a scandal? Then, who would dress her hair? And besides, Peg was with her. And, moreover, in the depths of her heart had not the young actress a secret desire to be left with her terrible lover, a wild longing mingled with fear, like that of the youthful soldier who anticipates with joy, yet dreads to enter, his first battle.

Casting aside her wraps the Quakeress quitted the dressing-room with a lively step, which suggested pretty Sarah Lightfoot rather than sedate Mrs. Marsham. The hair-dressing advanced rapidly, and although a trifle unsteady by reason of internal emotion, the young nobleman acquitted himself with marvellous distinction.

Although a simpler taste had begun to obtain, the *coiffure* of a woman of 1780 was still a remarkably complicated affair; so complicated, in fact, that certain women, by way of avoiding fatigue or expense, had their heads dressed only two or three times a week, sometimes only once, and slept in this heavy, uncomfortable, voluminous rigging, of which their own hair was assuredly the least important element. False hair being very costly, the interior of the fragile edifices was often stuffed with horsehair, and even with hay. In some cases a brace of iron wire was affixed to the head, upon which flowers, feathers, ribbons, and jewelry could be firmly attached; and thus the scaffolding frequently rose to such a height that, if we may credit the caricaturists of the day, it was necessary to pierce the roofs of the sedan-chairs, and even of the coaches, in order to accommodate *les élégantes* in gala costume.

However, there could be no question of such exaggeration in the case of a Shakespearean heroine. Of all the poet's creations is not Beatrice the most fantastic? And was not Esther, of all who had essayed the *rôle*, the most original in her style of beauty, the most unique in her method of playing it? That is why Mowbray, clearing all traditions at a single bound, had given free rein to his fancy. He had lowered the conventional scaffolding, cut short the tower-shaped *coiffure*. The top of the head was relieved, while two undulant, billowy masses depended therefrom, flowing behind the ears, no powder being used, which brought out at once the delicate contour and exquisite coloring of the face in strong relief. There was nothing classical nor rococo about it; it was all odd, novel, and overwhelmingly graceful. Esther had but to cast one glance at the mirror to be convinced that she had never been more beautiful.

Mowbray leaned towards the maid and whispered a word in her ear.

"What is it?" inquired Esther.

"Nothing," replied Mowbray; "Miss Peg is going in search of some pins which I require."

"Peg, I forbid you to leave the room!"

But the command came too late. Whether Peg had not heard or had seen fit not to hear, she had quitted the room. Scarcely had the door closed ere Mowbray stooped and murmured her name.

She had risen and recoiled across the room.

"Oh, my lord, this is wrong!" she cried.

"Mowbray's wish makes wrong right," he replied. "What do you fear,—the man who loves you to distraction?"

Resolutely she fixed her eyes on his, striving to read therein, beyond the disarray of his senses, the true thought which animated him.

"You love me? You have already said the same thing to twenty others,—to Bella Vereker, for instance!"

He shrugged his shoulders impatiently.

"I have never owned a second love! Neither she, nor any one else. You are my first love, and you shall be the only one!"

"I do not believe you. You are not telling me truth."

"Certainly I am," he exclaimed. "You shall be Lady Mowbray in the sight of God and man, with the reversion of the office which my mother holds at court."

This was no illusion! Esther began to weaken, vanity being in reality her vulnerable point.

At this moment a heavy knocking sounded upon the door, so resonant, so brutal that they both trembled.

"They are about to begin!" cried a voice in the passage. Perhaps it may seem singular to those who have not experienced similar situations, that such an incident can save a young girl; that the sentiment of secondary but immediate duty can brusquely awaken her at the moment that the notion of primal duty is losing its hold upon her. Esther recovered her presence of mind upon the instant.

"I am on in the first scene!" she cried. "Quick, my costume!"

She threw open the door. The callboy had disappeared, but one of the company who was to play the part of Hero, already dressed, was just descending to the greenroom.

"Are they beginning?" Esther demanded.

"Not yet."

"But I have just been called."

"Who could have done it? Some joke of course. You have a quarter of an hour yet."

"But I am alone!"

"Then I will help you."

During this dialogue Mowbray made good his escape. The blow had been struck! Who had struck it at the decisive moment? Who had dared to snatch his prey from him? Could it be Lebeau? He again! At the thought Mowbray's face grew dark with hatred.

CHAPTER IX.

MUCH ADO ABOUT NOTHING.

Slowly the curtain rose. In the great hall of the palace the good Lord Leonato, sovereign of a fantastic country which only Shakespeare knew, having at his two sides his daughter Hero and his niece Beatrice, with all his court about him, receives the messenger who comes to announce the victory of his troops and their imminent return.

Such is the spectacle from the auditorium; but the spectacle of the auditorium, seen from the stage, is otherwise curious; to modern eyes it would seem like a glimpse of fairyland.

A myriad candles shed from on high upon four thousand spectators a flood of soft, white light. The snowy wainscoting relieved with gold, the toilets of the men and women, the naked shoulders, the diamonds, the orders,—all seemed to stand forth in relief against the pervading brilliance. Soft pink, pearl-gray, pigeon-breast, sea-green, pale blue, violet, faint gold, the clear white of silk, the dull white of satin, the cream white of old laces, every shade which could reflect the light, are mingled in one delicious harmony. Through the silence which falls upon the audience the soft *frou-frou* of silk and the flutter of fans are alone audible. Every face is turned towards the stage, attentive, smiling, already charmed. In that age of extreme sociability one did not go to the theatre to enjoy individual, egotistical comfort in a corner, but to share in common a pleasure which increased by the fact that it was shared. Those were looked for at Drury Lane whom one had met at Almack's, at the Pantheon, at Ranelagh, those whom one had seen thirty years earlier at Vauxhall and Marylebone Gardens.

From a box Prince Orloff displays his gigantic figure, his diamonds, and his handsome face, which had vanquished a Czarina. It was here that an adroit pickpocket, only two years before, had failed to relieve him of his famous snuff-box, valued at a million francs.

Not far from him Lord Sandwich, the Jemmy Twitcher of the popular song and the *bête noir* of all London, appears quite consoled for the tragic death of his lady-love, Miss Reay, who had been assassinated within the year by an amorous clergyman. The grim figure of Charles James Fox looms in the back of another box, the front of which is occupied by the Duchess of Rutland and the Duchess of Devonshire, the irresistible Georgiana, who will soon become his election broker and buy up votes for him (*Honi soit qui mal y pense!*) at the price of a kiss.

A little farther away, following the circular rank of columns, sit the inseparable trio, Lady Archer, Lady Buckinghamshire and Mrs. Hobart, the three wild faro-players whom the Lord Chief Justice menaced with the pillory, and whom the caricaturist Gillray nailed there for all time. Lady Vereker has also come to applaud her little friend. In the second tier of boxes is enthroned Mrs. Robinson, fresh from teaching the Prince of Wales his first lesson in love. That man, whose fund of small-talk seems inexhaustible and insolent, but whose intelligent face catches every eye, is Sheridan, who has become director of Drury Lane by buying up Garrick's share. At his side lounges the exquisitely languid figure of a young woman, of late Miss Linley, the singer, now Mrs. Sheridan; for he has acquired her, thanks to his audacity, having run away with her in the face and eyes of her family and no end of suitors, while upon the adventure he has founded a comedy, the success of which is his wife's dowry.

In the gallery are seen more *beaux* than women, the *élégantes* and coxcombs, who are still termed *macaronis*, although the word is beginning to pass out of vogue. Rings, frills, and ruffles, the cut of coat and waistcoat, the latest suggestion in breeches,—all is with them a matter of profound meditation, from the buckle upon their shoes to the tip of their curled heads. Their hair is a mass of snow, conical in shape, about which floats the odor of iris and bergamot. Sellwyn, forever dreaming of his little marchioness, sits beside Reynolds, who holds his silver ear-trumpet towards the stage. Near them is Burgoyne, who consoles himself for his great military disaster at Saratoga by writing comedies. He has chosen the better part of the vanquished, which is to cry louder than anybody else and accuse everybody. For the one hundredth time he is explaining to Capt. Vancouver that the true author of the capitulation in America was not he, Burgoyne, who signed it, but that infernal Lord North, who gave the commands to the Liberal officers at Westminster in order to be rid of them, and then laughed in his sleeve at their reverses.

Before the royal box stand two Guards, armed from head to foot, immovable as statues. The king in his Windsor uniform, red with blue facings, his hair bound by a simple black ribbon, toys with a lorgnette, and leans his great awkward body forward with a curious and amused air. "Farmer George," though frequently cross and disagreeable, appears in excellent humor this evening. Undoubtedly his cabbage plants are doing well, or perhaps he has succeeded in making a dozen buttons during the day, since the manufacture of buttons and the culture of vegetables, which he sells to the highest bidder, are his favorite pastimes. Stiff and straight in her low-cut corsage, a true German in matters of etiquette, which she imposes with pitiless rigor upon all about her, little Queen Charlotte amply compensates for the free and easy habits of her husband by the severity of her mien. With head erect, though slightly thrown backward, squinting eyes, and pointed chin, swaying her fan to and fro with a rapid, uncompromising movement, there is no doubt that the worthy dwarf, who has already given the king thirteen princes and princesses, is still a most energetic little person.

On either side sit the Prince of Wales and Prince Frederick. The former realizes to the eye the type of the genuine Prince Charming, exquisite to a degree, but unsatisfactory with all his beauty, freshness and grace. The delicious envelope lacks soul. Later history will write against his name, "deceiver, perjurer and bigamist." But he is only eighteen years of age now, every heart is his, and yonder his first sweetheart regards him with ardent eyes. He takes no heed of it, however; in fact, a slight pout of annoyance sullies his otherwise delightful features. Prince Frederick is heir to the throne of Hanover, and his father's favorite. The destiny of that blockhead is to be duped by women, despised by his wife, and whipped by the French,—a fate which, nevertheless, has not denied him a triumphal statue perched upon the apex of a column, as though he had been a Trajan, a Nelson, or a Bonaparte.

In the shadow of the queen's chair is the tabouret of Lady Harcourt, her maid-of-honor and friend; while all in a row behind the princes stand the gentlemen-in-waiting.

Every one was in his place, including our friend, Mr. O'Flannigan. Installed in his hole, he held, spread out before him, a large portfolio containing the precious manuscript of the play, bearing erasures and corrections in Garrick's own hand.

A youthful voice, pure and vibrant, is heard, and the silence becomes still more profound. It is Beatrice who speaks by the mocking lips of Esther.

She requests news of Benedick from the messenger who has returned from the battle, but in the way that one would ask tidings of an enemy. Soon Benedick himself appears, whereupon begins a remarkable assault of sarcasm. Both provoke each other and defy love.

"I had rather hear my dog bark at a crow," she says, "than a man swear he loves me."

"God keep your ladyship still in that mind," retorts Benedick, "so some gentleman or other shall 'scape a predestinate scratched face."

"Scratching could not make it worse, an' 'twere such a face as yours were."

"Well, niece," says the uncle Leonato by and by, "I hope to see you one day fitted with a husband."

"Not till God make men of some other metal than earth. Would it not grieve a woman to be overmastered with a piece of valiant dust, to make an account of her life to a clod of wayward marl? No, uncle, I'll none; Adam's sons are my brethren, and truly I hold it a sin to match in my kindred." And later when they press her she replies:—

"He that hath a beard is more than a youth; and he that hath no beard is less than a man; and he that is more than a youth is not for me; and he that is less than a man I am not for him."

Don Pedro, the Prince of Arragon, sportively offers himself.

"Will you have me, lady?"

"No, my lord, unless I might have another for working-days; your grace is too costly to wear every day."

But, fearing that she has been guilty of an impertinence, she gently though still pertly excuses herself:—

"But I beseech your grace, pardon me; I was born to speak all mirth, and no matter."

"Out of question you were born in a merry hour!"

"No, sure, my lord, my mother cried; but, then, there was a star danced, and under that was I born."

"By my troth!" exclaims the Prince, wholly charmed, "a pleasant-spirited lady!"

Which was the opinion of all, both on the stage and off. Esther seemed to have forgotten the danger she had run, the emotion she had experienced; or, rather, this danger and emotion lent to her eyes and voice a lively, incisive charm of gayety and extraordinary audacity. She was the very embodiment of that wit "quick as the greyhound's mouth," which forms the motive of the play. The quips and cranks of the poet seemed born upon her lips with the freedom and supreme grace of improvisation, and if here and there there occur certain rather weak or coarse sallies, she allowed the audience no time to perceive them. It was a rain, a very hail-storm which fell upon the heads of Benedick, Leonato, and Don Pedro, mixed with blinding lightning. With a glance of the eye she addressed her most trenchant words to Mowbray, whom she descried standing at the back of the Prince of Wales's chair. But it was surely no longer against him that she defended herself, since she felt herself assailed by every one in the theatre. She pitted herself against the game with elation. She no longer played a part, but was herself; she was no exceptional creature, but a young English girl of all times, who accosts love with a mocking air, though with a beating heart, with defiance upon her lips, backed by a pretty, mutinous insolence and a belligerent effervescence of words. Upon this battlefield of love, like her brothers in veritable combats, she had no wish to bite the dust. Though vanquished, she knows it not.

There was a genuine sigh, a shudder throughout the auditorium, when Beatrice, deceived by stratagem and thrown off her guard, bows her head and gives vent to those charming words:—

"'Contempt, farewell! and maiden pride, adieu!'"

Fate is a strange manipulator of effects! At the moment that she raised her eyes her glance met that of a young man who stood at the back of the *parterre*, pallid with emotion; it was Francis Monday! Then they saw their Beatrice wholly transformed; moved, vibrant, saddened. How well she understood the grief of her cousin Hero, unjustly suspected by her bethrothed! Now that she loved, how swiftly her heart divined and sympathized with the pangs of love! With what a burst of pity, sympathy, and feminine heroism she cried:—

"'Oh, that I were a man for his sake! or that I had any friend would be a man for my sake! But manhood is melted into courtesies, valor into compliment, and men are only turned into tongue, and trim ones too: he is now as valiant as Hercules that only tells a lie, and swears it.—I cannot be a man with wishing, therefore I will die a woman with grieving.'"

Then with a short sob she fell upon a chair. Suffering and joy,—she had traversed the whole domain o'er which woman reigns. Those tears consecrated the defeat of Beatrice, the triumph of Esther.

The audience burst into rapturous applause, and when the play was over the young actress was informed that his Majesty desired to see her.

Thereupon she was conducted to the royal box, or, rather, to the reception room which adjoined it. The gentlemen-in-waiting made way for her, and in the space left vacant, the cynosure of every eye, the young girl paused for a moment confused.

"Approach, Miss Woodville," said her Majesty with that German accent which has been the butt of so many pleasantries.

Esther advanced a step or two, and then sank in a profound courtesy.

"Ah! ah! Miss Woodville. Charmed to see you and to congratulate you!"

It was the king who spoke. He came to her with that inimitable gait, upon which the circus-clowns of the day wasted study and art in their attempts to reproduce it, but which in his Majesty was natural. He held his body bent like a half-moon, the back arched, the legs down to the knees pressed close together, and the feet wide apart. Being upon the point of leaving the theatre before the little piece which terminated the performance, he already held his gloves in one hand, his cane in the other, and his hat under his arm. Upon reaching the spot where Esther stood he let fall his gloves. She stooped to pick them up, while he, wishing to spare her the exertion, dropped his cane; quickly seizing it, he lost his hold upon his hat. Thereupon ensued a moment of confusion, which the queen, in an attempt to abridge, made use of by addressing a compliment to the young artist.

"You are Garrick's last pupil, I believe," she said, "and perhaps his best. He would have been happy indeed to have heard you this evening."

"Eh? what? Garrick?" gasped his Majesty. "Oh, certainly, certainly! She plays remarkably well. I'm a judge myself: I too have played in comedy—comedy and tragedy. I used to do Addison's 'Cato,' and not half badly, they said. But of course one always says that to a prince. Have you seen 'Cato,' Miss Woodville?"

"Never, sire."

"Ah, but it is a fine play! And the tirade, the famous tirade, you know!"

And he began to declaim, floundering for words. Again her Majesty interrupted him, although with every demonstration of respect.

"Does not your Majesty find that Miss Woodville speaks her Shakespeare marvellously well?"

"Eh? what? Shakespeare? Of course!—You love Shakespeare, do you not?"

"Oh, yes, sire, with all my heart!"

"That's right; so do I. Nevertheless he has his stupid absurdities. Sad rubbish, some of it. Persons generally would not venture to admit that they thought so, but I say it because I say whatever comes into my mind. I don't care particularly for the French, but I am forced to acknowledge that their plays are the noblest, most decorous and normal extant. We also have good authors, such as Coleman, for instance, or Mr. Home, who wrote 'Douglass.' The whole action of the play passes in twenty-four hours and in one and the same place. Certain scenes take place in the castle, others before the castle, and still others behind the castle; but, in a word, the castle is always there to preserve the unity. That makes you laugh, young woman!"

In fact, the king himself laughed too.

"All the same," he concluded in a paternal tone, "you play like an angel!"

"*Au revoir*, Miss Woodville," said the queen; "I take it your Majesty wishes to be going."

The audience was at an end, and after a second courtesy Esther backed herself out of the presence. Upon the threshold her glance met that of Lord Mowbray, and she thought that upon his arm she might penetrate this grand world, not as she had just done, for a few moments, but forever,—forever to hold her place and rank in the charmed circle!

CHAPTER X.

DEATH TO THE PAPISTS.

There was ever the same contrast between the component parts of Esther's dual existence: after fairyland the humble, prosaic existence. A few days after that triumphal evening Esther found herself alone at the end of the garden, embroidery in hand. The little terrace upon which she had seated herself was enclosed by a breast-high wall. Above this wall a trellis covered with vines and climbing plants would have formed on that side an impenetrable screen, had not large oval apertures been managed whence a view of the surrounding country could be secured. Laying her work aside, Esther leaned upon her elbows and took a survey of Tothill Fields, where several groups of men ran hither and thither with cries, playing at bowls and football. In the distance a gray veil glimmered above the river, which, though invisible, could easily be traced. Behind the roofs of Chelsea Hospital undulated the verdant masses of Battersea Park. To the right, above the old clock tower of Kensington, the westering sun was sinking tranquilly to rest. A few yards away a band of gypsies had encamped for the night. The half-naked children played in the sun, while the women were hanging out their linen to dry. The old men, immovable as statues, crouched in the shade, smoked their pipes, keeping their eyes on their unharnessed horses, which browsed upon the sparse herbage.

One of the gypsy women wandered near the terrace, and with a smile slowly approached Esther. Tall, well-built, with a flat, sun-burned face, glossy black hair, and bold, piercing eyes of a strange fixity of glance, and conspicuous by the utter absence of soul in their depths, she regarded Esther with a curious scrutiny. She leaned her back against the dry trunk of an old willow and balanced herself, not without a certain savage grace, which displayed her muscular limbs to advantage beneath the rags which covered them.

"A fine day," said she, "for such as cherish love in their hearts."

"Love! Nonsense!" sneered Esther.

"She who speaks thus is generally caught in the toils."

"Can you tell fortunes?"

"Give me your hand and you shall see."

"Oh, yes, I know you; you gypsies are all alike. For sixpence you announce the love of a city clerk; for a shilling, it is a gentleman; for half a crown, a lord; were one to give you a goldpiece, it would be a prince!"

"What would you say," said the woman roughly, "were I to tell your fortune for nothing? Only beware: I shall tell it, good or bad!—Ah! you start. You *do* believe!"

"Here is my hand," said Esther, moved despite herself.

But stretch and lengthen her arm as she would, her hand only reached the gypsy's eyes.

"Wait!" she cried, and, running lightly round to a little postern gate, she threw it open, and found herself face to face with the stranger, who for some moments held the white, tapering fingers in her great, strong, brown hand.

"Well?"

"Your life-line is well marked, but it is crossed here."

"Some danger?"

"A great crisis."

"At what epoch?"

"If I had drawn up your horoscope, I could have told you almost to an hour. So far as I can see, it will occur before your eighteenth year is accomplished."

"I shall be eighteen next Friday!"

"In that case the hour approaches. Be prepared. I see something else. Several men love you."

"How can you see that in my hand?"

"Child! I am reading your mind at this moment; it is like an open book to me."

Esther would have withdrawn her hand, but that she felt it imprisoned as in a vise. The woman stood erect and rigid before her, her eye vitreous, with difficulty expelling her breath between her half open lips. At last she spoke as one in a dream.

"There are three! One is dressed in black."

"Reuben!" murmured Esther.

"The other is a fine gentleman."

"And the third?"

"The third! I cannot distinguish his features.—Yes,—now I see him!—Why, how singular!"

"Why?"

"He resembles the second!"

"Ah!"

"And he holds in his hand—"

"What does he hold?"

"A pencil, I think; yes, he is an artist."

After a brief pause she resumed,—

"Two of these men will soon disappear, but the worthiest will marry you and you will be a great lady."

A flash of pride illumined Esther's eyes.

"Should your prophesy be realized," she said, "seek me out, and I will give you this ring which you see upon my hand."

"I do not want your ring; give me rather the handkerchief which you hold."

"Why do you wish this valueless thing? Is it that you are my well-wisher? Do you love me?"

"I hate you, as I hate all Christians; but I have need, for an incantation, of an object which has belonged to a virgin."

As Esther hesitated, the gypsy snatched the filmy tissue from her hand and fled, vanishing round an angle in the wall like an apparition.

Considerably disturbed in mind, Esther remained some time motionless upon the spot where the gypsy had left her. It seemed to her that the strange creature had exhaled a sort of torpor which she could not shake off. At last she closed the gate and stepped back. As she did so she noticed a bit of folded paper lying at her feet and picked it up. Unfolding it, she read these lines:—

"You love me. I feel it, know it. Have confidence in my love and honor. I long to tear you from the slavery in which you live to dwell with me in brightness and joy. Go to the Pantheon on Friday next wearing a brown domino with blue rosettes, and when you hear behind you these words, 'The moon is risen,' directly leave the person who will accompany you and follow the one who will take your hand. Ir order to assure me that you consent, send me some article which you have worn. I cannot be mistaken in the scent of vervain, which you love. While inhaling it, it will seem as though I inhaled your breath, as though I held my Esther in my arms."

No address, no signature. But the origin of the missive was no more doubtful than its destination.

"How stupid have I been!" exclaimed the girl. "Of what a farce have I been the dupe! Here I fancied that I was dealing with a sorceress, and she turns out to be a common go-between! It was she who dropped this letter at my feet. Out of doubt she knew its contents. That is why she snatched my handkerchief, for which she will be well paid;—and all the while I was wondering at her disinterestedness!"

With a twinge of vexation she thought that even at that moment Lord Mowbray probably believed that he held the pledge of his victory.

"Bah!" she mentally ejaculated; "what matters it? His triumph will be short-lived, since I will not go to the masquerade on Friday; though I could go if I wished. Lady Vereker and my theatre companions have wished to take me there. Reuben has had only one word to say upon the abominations of the Pantheon, and my aunt, who is afraid of him, has been only too ready to refuse her permission. But there is nothing to fear!"

Just a shade of disappointment and annoyance dimmed this reassuring thought, but an unexpected incident altered the face of the matter. Reuben was absent at tea-time. He had scarcely been visible for several days; he appeared to be wholly absorbed in projects of import, of which he disclosed no hint to any one.

"My dear child," said Mrs. Marsham with a touch of embarrassment and some mystery, "I have undertaken a surprise for you which it is quite time to reveal. For a long time you have desired to see a masked ball at the Pantheon, but as I dare not entrust you to the care of so frivolous a person as your new friend, Lady Vereker, I have decided to take you there myself."

"You, aunt!"

"Why not? To the pure all things are pure, and if my eyes commit the sin of looking upon evil, I shall at least have the consolation of screening your innocence from the dangerous spectacle. Moreover, I shall pray without ceasing, and the Lord will go with us."

"But we really ought to have a different sort of cavalier."

"I have thought of that, and have asked Mr. O'Flannigan to serve as our escort. He is a brave man, as he has amply proved himself to be. We shall have, in case of an emergency, an intrepid defender. He has consented, and all that remains is for us to prepare our costumes."

Good Mrs. Marsham forgot to add that, like her niece, she was dying to see a masked ball, and that the curiosity which had been devouring her for years played its little part in the famous "surprise."

"Above all things," she added, "not a word to Reuben!"

When at last she found herself alone in her chamber Esther could not but reflect upon the odd situation which was hurrying on towards a dangerous result. After all, she was free to go to the Pantheon, and even to wear a brown domino with blue rosettes, without its leading to anything culpable. Her heart beat, and she experienced that delicious vertigo which conducts the great-granddaughters of Eve to the verge of the abyss.

What should she do? Of whom ask advice? She had neither mother nor friend, at least no friend who merited the name. Under similar circumstances gamblers toss up a goldpiece; bigots open the Scriptures and the first verse upon which their eyes fall resolves their doubt after the manner of an oracle. At the moment she was standing before a table upon which rested a bust of Shakespeare with a vase of flowers, a sort of offering renewed each day as though it were a domestic altar. A book-shelf upon the wall contained the works of the great dramatist. In those pages, so often conned, Esther had learned to think and to feel, to know mankind, the world, and love. It was her Bible, her book of books, august and authentic revelation before all others, the repository of her religion and philosophy. For this reason, struck with a sudden inspiration, she caught up the volume, which opened of itself to the first scene of the second act of "All's Well That Ends Well." In the middle of the page five words seemed to blaze before her stupefied eyes,—

"*By Heaven, I'll steal away!*"

There was no ambiguity in this response. Esther bowed her head as if overwhelmed by a fatality. At this moment the memory of Frank crossed her mind. Again she saw that sweetly sad face with eyes which reproached her for her treason. She felt an inward anguish; it seemed to her that, following the example of the pirates of the Thames, whose cruelty she had so lately condemned, she was casting the poor boy a second time into the dark abyss that yawned to engulf him.

But she rose with a sort of rage against the thought. Had Frank ever spoken a word of love to her? Did she even know that he loved her?

And her conscience promptly replied,—

"Yes, you do know; his eyes have told you!"

Well, so be it; he did love her; but could she consider a man who possessed nothing, whose profession earned him scarce a livelihood? Could she marry her poverty to Frank's misery? She saw herself as if depicted in two different pictures. Here, wretched, faded before her time, nursing a puny infant in a garret, bare of even the necessaries of life. In the companion picture, covered with diamonds and flowers, she was entering St James's, while the gentlemen-in-waiting bowed before her and a footman announced, "Lady Mowbray!"

When Mrs. Marsham inquired, "What will your domino be?" she answered, "Brown with blue ribbons."

That same evening aunt and niece set out for Drury Lane as usual, leaving Maud asleep in the kitchen. The shades of night had begun to gather about the little house in Tothill Fields,—a calm, balmy night towards the end of May. The strollers had gone their ways, and the gypsy camp had emigrated to another of the great tracts of waste land so numerous at that day in the suburbs of London. Save the distant rumbling from Westminster naught disturbed the peace of this countrified quarter, already dozing in the evening silence. Nevertheless, several shadows flitted along the old wall; men in groups of two and three made their way noiselessly towards the little postern gate where Esther had conversed with the gypsy. A lantern placed upon the threshold guided them towards the narrow entrance veiled in ivy. After a minute or two, which seemed carefully calculated, a new group followed the one that preceded it. Once within the garden the men seemed to hesitate, wandering here and there haphazard in the dense obscurity of the old trees. Presently Reuben's voice called to them:—

"This way, brothers!"

Thereupon they followed him, descended a stairway of seven or eight steps, and penetrated a vaulted hall, where they found all those who had preceded them united. The floor was of well-trodden earth, while the walls bore numerous traces of mould. There was nothing in the way of furniture except a few wooden benches, a table at the back, and a single lamp suspended from the ceiling, the ruddy flame of which flickered with every gust of air above their heads.

When the assembly was complete Reuben carefully closed the doors. At this moment the chamber contained some twenty men. Two among them were attired in clerical garb, but with that extreme simplicity which marked the members of dissenting churches. The remainder appeared to be either shop-keepers or laborers. Some even were in their working clothes, notably a tanner with his leathern apron, and a butcher with his knife hanging from his belt. One man only was attired with elegance, although the tints were sombre. His little narrow head and thin, pale face, feminine in outline, emerged from an aureole of powdered hair, and were illumined by a pair of eyes singularly close together, black, glittering, and hard, and animated by an expression of inquietude. His companions treated him with marked respect, and seemed to be of one mind in yielding him first place in everything. They addressed him as "Lord George"; in fact, he was Lord George Gordon, a Scotch nobleman, who had begun to attract attention in the House of Commons by his peculiarities. After a term of years spent in dissipation, folly, and travelling, he served in the navy, demanded a post of command from the ministry, failed to obtain it, and suddenly joined the opposition. Again, quite as brusquely changing his tactics, he put himself at the head of a party of intolerants who were opposing the repeal of the laws against the Catholics.

Lord George Gordon took his place behind the table, with one of the clergymen upon his right hand and Reuben on his left.

"Friends," he began in a very sweet and modulated tone, "our host, this worthy young man, who is animated by the spirit of God,—our friend Reuben Marsham,—informs me that an indelible memory attaches to this chamber in which we are met. When the impious Charles Stuart remounted the throne of which his father had been deprived by the anger of the Lord, and which the weakness of men had restored to the son, two fugitives were concealed here, and lived for a considerable time in this subterranean hall, existed here until, through the information of a servant, their asylum was discovered. The tyrant's soldiery dragged them forth, and they lost their heads upon the scaffold, praising God, who held their rewards in store for them. Shades of the great dead, martyrs of the holy cause, here do I salute your invisible presence! Be with us! Inspire, protect us!"

A tremor passed through the very bones of each auditor. Thereupon the clergyman took up the word.

"Since we are assembled for the glory of God and of His Son, let us first invoke his most holy name, my brothers; let us pray!"

He fell upon his knees; every man imitated his example with such unanimous precision that the earth gave forth a dull sound, as when at the word of command a company of soldiers grounds arms.

The clergyman intoned in a low voice the psalm beginning, "By the rivers of Babylon."

To each verse all present murmured a response, toning their rough, harsh voices. When the last *amen* had been pronounced Lord George remarked, "Friends, none among us is ignorant of our purpose in coming hither to-night. For the sake of those of us who have not been present at our previous reunions, I will in brief rehearse the facts. Aided by a damnable philosophy, impiety has made great progress in our midst, disguised at present under the new name of tolerance. Thanks to these circumstances, Rome has reared her head. The great courtesan seeks to queen it among us with unveiled face and lofty brow. Sons of the saints, will you permit it?"

"No!" responded twenty voices.

"You are aware that a bill has been presented to the House of Commons annulling the penal laws against the Catholics. I have raised my voice in protest, but my words have been choked in my throat and I have been treated as a fool. Both parties are united against us!"

Varied exclamations greeted these words.

"Burke is a Jesuit in disguise!"

"Fox is a scapegrace, a drunkard, a gambler!"

"Lord North's only thought is to fill his pockets and his stomach!"

"The Parliament is rotten to the core!"

"We must appeal to the king!" cried one.

"I have thought of that," said Lord George, "and I brought him one of the pamphlets which I have published on the subject. His Majesty listened to a part of it, and promised to read the rest. That was many months ago, and still I have no response from him."

"The king," observed the clergyman upon Gordon's right, "has no power to interfere in the resolutions of Parliament and in the legal vote."

"Is he prevented," burst out Reuben impetuously, "when some policy of his own is at stake, or when he wishes to depose some minister who has displeased him?"

Thereupon the tanner boldly advanced.

"The king is playing us false!" said he. "A while ago he went to dinner with Lord Petre. Now, do you know who this Lord Petre is? A determined papist! He is the grand-nephew of that same Father Petre who brought to the palace in a warming-pan that miller's son whom they presented as the Prince of Wales, and whom they have since called the knight of Saint George!"

"That's neither here nor there."

"Wait!" continued the tanner with unruffled obstinacy. "When one is the friend of a papist, one is nigh to becoming a papist. Who knows whether the king is not already baptized!"

"It is certain in any case," interrupted Reuben, "that we have only ourselves to depend upon. Unless we intimidate the House of Commons the law will be passed."

"Yes," assented Lord George, "that is the truth. I have given notice that on Friday I intend to lay our petition before Parliament, and that I shall have two hundred thousand men to back me. You don't propose to fail me, do you?"

"Certainly not!" cried the clergyman. "Each one of us is good for ten thousand; we will answer for our neighborhoods."

"Will the Methodists march?" inquired Reuben.

"Every mother's son of them," replied a voice. "John Wesley has declared against tolerance."

"In that case," said Gordon, "success is assured. We will meet at Saint George's Fields at ten o'clock; there the final arrangements will be made. Neglect no detail, brothers, which will tend to make our manifestation imposing, grand, and irresistible. Infiltrate every soul with the fire which animates you. Let the voice of the people, which is the voice of God, be heard. For a century pious England has slept, lulled by the indifference of mechanical practices, mercantile preoccupations, ambitious intrigues, and worldly pleasures. The sun of the morrow should shine upon her awakening, and this awakening should be so sudden, so powerful, as to terrify the enemies of God. Let our warcry be that of our ancestors, 'To your tents, O Israel!'"

"Brothers," said the clergyman in his turn, "let us intone the song of the Hebrews, when God delivered them out of the land of Egypt,—*Cantemus Domino!*"

They sang, always *sotto voce*, but the sustained accent of those deep voices lent to the terrible words their full energy.

"O God, thou hast crushed thine enemies. The sea has swallowed them up;

they have fallen into the depths like a stone. Thou hast sent thine anger upon them; it has consumed them like straw. The enemy hath said, I will pursue them, I will fall upon them, I will share their spoils, I will slay them with my sword, and I will be master. But thou hast sent thy breath upon them, and they have been swallowed up as lead in a raging sea. O Lord, what God is like unto thee!"

They sang, and a very tempest of enthusiasm whistled among their bowed heads. A sort of heroic madness raised their commonplace souls quite out of themselves. They fancied that they felt the spirit of the Lord upon them; not the God of pity, who blesses and pardons, raises the fallen, makes the sinner a saint, wipes away tears, heals the wounded, promises peace to the weary, glory to the humble, love to the forsaken, heaven to all such as the earth has wounded and made desperate, but a powerful, jealous, revengeful God, a God who seeks bloody holocausts, and pursues in the children the sins of the father, in the infant at the breast the iniquities of vanished generations.

"The day of glory is at hand!" cried Reuben. "Happy are they who perish in the combat!"

"Amen!" was the universal response.

And with that word they dispersed.

CHAPTER XI.

THE DAY OF DAYS.

A cloudless sun rose upon the 2d of June, 1780. Before six o'clock a large crowd filled Saint George's Fields and the neighborhood. A certain number of the men sought each other and stood in groups as if in obedience to a previous word of command. They talked together in low tones and wore a sombre air of resolution. A great number of humble folk and shop-keepers had come hither at the request of their clergymen, convinced that they were destined to do a pious work in repulsing the religious joke of which their fathers had rid themselves; though from their very bearing it was evident that these worthies were ready to do more barking than biting. A multitude of the curious surrounded them, resolved to see the show out, though it should cost them a cracked pate or two. Occasionally a face betrayed fierce expectation of disorder, a sort of presentiment of what might occur; but the great day still hung heavily on their hands, and the men felt that their hour had not yet come, and that they must leave it to the psalm-singers and idlers to lead the way. About eleven o'clock Lord George Gordon appeared, and was received with acclamation. Mounted upon a table, he delivered some words which were quite lost, but his desperately energetic gestures were seen and were responded to with cries of "Down with popery!" "Death to the papists!"

The leaders passed from place to place endeavoring to enforce order in this vast assemblage of men animated by such contrasting sentiments, but scarcely had they turned their backs ere the confusion was renewed. At last they succeeded in forming four main bodies, which, taking different ways, crossed the Thames upon three bridges,—Westminster, Blackfriars, and London Bridge.

At the head of this last column marched Reuben Marsham, whose fine, menacing face, flashing eyes, and floating yellow locks attracted universal attention, especially among the women. Men bore before him several banners upon which was emblazoned the legend, "No popery!" Behind came a silent phalanx of fanatical sectarians, who ordered their marching-step to the slow measures of a religious chant. The crowd followed in clamorous disorder, struggling with a thousand emotions, like a tempestuous flood-tide sweeping between the walls of the narrow streets. From the windows and the thresholds of the shops a curious, amused, but perfectly peaceful horde of people watched the progress of the procession.

Here and there a philosopher or practical man would shrug his shoulders, murmuring, "Fanatics!" or, "Still another working day wasted!" But the majority sympathized with the object of the expedition, and saluted the passage of the manifesto with answering cries of "No popery!"

No effort was made to interfere with the proceedings; not a red-coat nor an officer of police appeared. What could all the watchmen in London—those timid, innocent watchmen—have availed against such a multitude, even though they had been united in one solid troop? As for the soldiers, they were only called out as a last resort.

Reuben crossed Ludgate Hill without obstacle, went up Fleet Street, and, having passed through old Temple Bar, entered the Strand. As a river receives its affluents, the column constantly grew larger through the human currents which joined it from the north and swept into it from the side-streets. In front of houses where well-known Catholics dwelt the procession would pause while, amidst groans and cries of execration from the crowd, men slashed the doors with a chalk-mark, which designated the places for approaching vengeance.

Having followed the Strand to its end, traversed Charing Cross, and passed through Whitehall, the procession spread over Westminster Place, which, despite its somewhat confined dimensions and the buildings which obstructed it, nevertheless offered a favorable stamping-ground for such popular displays. The other bodies had already arrived at the rendezvous, and being united formed an immense, compact mass which nothing could resist. The crowd, proud of its power, gave voice to a long acclamation, above which isolated voices were heard, and which caused every window in Westminster to rattle.

The afternoon being far advanced, the hour of the meeting approached. The members of the two assemblies who had not taken time by the forelock and reached the House of Parliament were recognized as they courageously tried to penetrate the crowd, were marked out, abused, and beaten; but the popular hatred was particularly directed against the orators, ministers, and prelates, who were roundly accused, as they made their appearance, of betraying the cause of religion and of selling England to the Pope. With their carriage windows broken, their horses wildly snorting, their coachmen purple with rage or pallid with fear and deprived of their whips and reins, their terrified footmen clinging to the straps behind, the coaches swayed like ships in distress upon this furious human sea. They cracked and oscillated, until it was quite a wonder they were not overturned. The unfortunate occupants were torn from their seats and dragged over the pavements by the legs, arms, and even by their powdered cues. "Kill them! Drown them!" was the cry. Lord North, Lord Sandwich, the Archbishop of York, and several others thus saw imminent death staring them in the face, and escaped it only by their presence of mind or the energy of their friends. The crowd grew intoxicated with success, but more particularly with the gin and the beer which were dispensed in floods by the publicans of the neighborhood. Who could foretell to what point of excess the affair would be carried?

One after another the members of Parliament succeeded in joining their colleagues. With their frills and ruffles in streamers, soiled with mud and blood, they bore ample testimony of the violence to which they had been subjected. Each one regarded the event according to his particular humor; some laughed and swore, while others, grinding their teeth and pale with rage, silently wiped their faces where they had been wounded by the missiles, or their lacerated ears, which dripped blood upon their fine attire. All these men bore the sword; many had used it; the majority had risked their lives for a trifle in worldly duels, genuine tilting scrimmages with bare bodkins. They had no fear of a London rabble; the instinct of battle, the taste for combat, which is never quite dormant in the breast of an Englishman, awoke within them. One very aged member recounted how, sixty years before, the gentlemen of the Loyal Societies, whom a Jacobite mob of 1720 undertook to prevent from drinking King George's health, had charged upon the crowd in Cheapside and Fleet Street and had broken not a few worthless skulls. The recollection caused the old man's eyes to dance and excited the group of his more youthful hearers. "What say you if we make an onslaught?" proposed one of them.

With brandished canes a dozen of the younger members fell suddenly upon the multitude and disengaged a friend from his perilous situation. Several times was this manœuvre repeated, with visible pleasure on the part of those who executed it. What sport it was to warm the rascals' backs! Directly their canes did not suffice, they drew their swords and let a little blood for the good of their patients. Each time that this occurred the populace fell back with a howl to give them place out of respect for their quality, but instantly closed in again more furious than ever. Soon with that destructive power of crowds it had broken down the gates which had been closed against them, and had invaded the courtyard; even now it had surged to the foot of the staircase. Separated from the insurgents by only a few steps, the deputies, crowded together in a solid mass, stamped with rage the vestibule leading to the House. From time to time a member of the government would come to take a bird's-eye view of the state of affairs, as a sailor watches the weather, and would then return to the Treasurer's office and report to his colleagues.

Nathaniel Wraxall, who had travelled everywhere, conspired with a queen, risked his head in various countries, and had been mixed up in all the brawls of his time, stood leaning upon the balustrade, watching the spectacle with the calmly profound scrutiny of an entomologist at his microscope. He listened to the remarks, studied the faces, and took mental notes for the edification of posterity. From time to time he would draw forth his watch, a beautiful work of art purchased in Paris, which struck the hours and played the chimes of Dunkirk at noon and midnight, in order not to make any error in the chronology of the different phases of the day. If the precincts of Parliament, violated by Cromwell and his Round-heads, but unassailed unto the present time by vulgar invasion, were fated to be profaned by the mob, it was important that Wraxall should be able to state historically at what precise moment the fact was accomplished.

At this moment Lord George Gordon, borne in triumph upon the shoulders of the people, and accompanied by a deafening tumult, mounted the staircase. He was received with a burst of violent exclamations. His colleagues apostrophized him, seized him by the arms, and called upon him to order back the crowd. Without paying the slightest heed, Lord George, with his eternal smile upon his face and as calm as possible, very gently remarked:—

"By your leave, gentlemen."

Thereupon they followed him into the hall. With its vaulted ceiling, its sombre woodwork richly carved, its Gothic ornamentation and fine stained glass, which represented the story of Adam and Eve, together with that of the patriarchs and the principal events in the life of Christ, the ancient chapel of St. Stephen still preserved its religious character. Therein Parliament had sat for upwards of one hundred and twenty years. To be sure, it had not echoed the voices of Sir Thomas More and Bacon, but it had vibrated to the accents of Shaftesbury, of Bolingbroke, and the elder Pitt, and it still preserved the echoes of those noble harangues which Voltaire declared worthy of the Roman senate. Just then the silence which reigned within contrasted strangely with the infernal tumult outside. At the usual hour prayer had been said, the speaker had taken his seat, and the mace, that "plaything" of which Cromwell spoke so disdainfully, had been laid upon the table, which indicated the official opening of the meeting. The ministers upon their long, high-backed bench at the right hand of the speaker, the leaders of the opposition upon the opposite bench, the sergeant-at-arms standing just beyond the bar, the clerk seated at the table,—every one was at his post, as tranquil as though nothing out of the common were taking place.

Lord George Gordon demanded and obtained permission to lay upon the table a petition from the inhabitants of London who protested against the favors accorded to the Catholics.

"Two hundred thousand citizens have accompanied me in order to bear respectful witness," he said.

A bitter burst of sneering interrupted him, but Lord George repeated his phrase,—

"In order to bear respectful but firm witness of their immutable, unreserved devotion to the liberty acquired by their fathers at the cost of almost superhuman efforts."

Having pronounced these words he retired, taking special care to salute the speaker at the exact spot where this formality is expected.

Again the hall was nearly deserted, the members crowding out into the vestibule. Gordon reappeared and the vociferations were renewed. The maledictions and menaces from above were answered by an enthusiastic clamor from below. The tumult assumed such proportions that a man speaking in his neighbor's ear and using the whole power of his lungs was unable to make himself understood. Believing that Gordon was about to join his friends, they barred his passage.

"You are a hostage," they said, "and you shall not go out!"

Lord George made a sign that he had no idea of going; he only desired to speak a few encouraging words to the crowd. He descended a few steps and attempted to speak, but all that was heard were such fragments as: "Cause of God ... generous martyrs ... detestable idolatry ... rights of the people ... even unto death."

Finding that his voice failed to prevail against the noise, he returned to his colleagues; whereupon the multitude prepared to follow him. Then Col. Gordon, who was a relative of the young lord, but of quite a different calibre, drew his sword.

"You see!" he exclaimed. "Now I swear to you, sir, that if one of these wretches enters here you are a dead man! Before he crosses the threshold of Parliament I shall have passed my sword through your body!"

The little sleek, colorless face preserved its slyly evil smile. He scarcely blinked his eyes before the tempest of furious insults which burst upon him.

"The villains!" cried Reuben. "They are going to murder him!"

Drawing a pistol from his mantle, he was about to rush forward, when the roll of drums was heard. It was Col. Woodford with a detachment of the Guards coming to the relief of Parliament.

The crowd recoiled step by step, without panic or disorder, but with a dull muttering of hate which presaged a lively resistance. As for the soldiers, they advanced with precaution, content to occupy the abandoned ground and to rescue the gates. From all sides a rain of invective poured upon them, and even stones thrown from a distance fell within the ranks.

"Are you going to fight for the Pope now?" cried one; while another added,—

"Is it with the blood of Englishmen that the cardinals' gowns are dyed?"

The soldiers appeared crestfallen, disgusted with the part they were obliged to play. These fine fair-weather soldiers, who are rarely sent to war, relished still less the repression of a riot; and somehow the rumor passed from mouth to mouth that they were about to revolt, to refuse to obey their officers.

Within the Houses of Parliament a sudden change had taken place. If some of the members rejoiced at the deliverance, others murmured threat. The presence of the soldiers in the precincts of the representatives of the nation seemed to them a violation of the rights of Parliament almost as grave as had been the vulgar invasion. One phrase, always magical under such circumstances, circulated among them,—"Breach of privilege." The danger being passed, or at least avoided, the sentiment of justice towards and respect for the person of every citizen took its place. After all, these men who protested against the resolutions of the legislators were but using their right, albeit in rather buoyant fashion. Were they going to massacre them? Fists, canes and the flat of swords did not count, but gunshots were quite another matter! No, no: it was wiser to save the powder for the Frenchmen.

Night was closing in upon the field of battle. Their spirits were beginning to flag, for spirits cannot continue keyed up to a high pitch forever, and the most critical situations in great popular movements frequently languish for the reason that they have been too long sustained. The supper hour was keenly appreciated by every stomach, especially by those who had given themselves no time for dinner. Judge Addington profited by these circumstances to make an attempt at conciliation.

"Friends," he cried, "give me your word of honor that you will retire and I will dismiss the soldiers!"

A burst of applause followed the words. The Guards made ready to beat a retreat. A louder burst of applause. Considering that they had manifested their power and given their betters a lesson, the mob slowly evacuated the neighborhood of Parliament. By degrees the cries grew more indistinct, and at last Westminster Place was deserted. Both parties fancied themselves conquerors, and order appeared to be re-established.

This illusion was of short duration. A few minutes later prolonged cries, and flames which suddenly burst forth, reddening the heavens, announced the fact that the true excesses had but just begun. It soon became known that the populace had attacked the chapel of the Sardinian ambassador in Duke Street, and still another of the Romish persuasion in Warwick Street. Benches, pictures, chairs, crucifixes, and confessionals,—all had been torn down and dragged out of doors, leaving merely the four walls standing, and a bonfire was made of these instruments of idolatry. Menaced upon every hand, the Catholics fled in hot haste, as if London in the midst of the eighteenth century was about to assist at a Protestant "Saint Bartholomew."

Thus alarm reigned in one quarter of the town, while joy presided in another. While the shrieks of death resounded in Duke Street, they were dancing at the Pantheon!

CHAPTER XII.

THE MASQUERADE AT THE PANTHEON.

The two women had passed the entire day in arranging their dominos. Only an occasional echo of the popular disturbance had reached them; and when they learned that a great crowd had surrounded Parliament, Mrs. Marsham, who was not easily disquieted, remarked: "That's good! It is the petition against the papists." And she dismissed the subject from her mind once and for all.

As for Esther, a great calm had replaced her agitation of the preceding evening. The gypsy's prediction, the Shakespearean oracle, together with the conspiracy of things in general so far as her vanity was concerned, failed to prevail against the sentiment hidden away in the depths of her heart. She had arrived at a determination and proposed to abide by it. She would go to the ball, would have as pleasant a time as she could, but she would not permit herself to be led away. She would not notice any such preconcerted signal as "The moon is risen!" She was resolved to act thus—unless at the last minute, and actuated by some new caprice, she did exactly the contrary.

Esther was ready in good time, and Mrs. Marsham, although much slower, was not behind hand in joining her in the parlor.

About nine o'clock, shortly after nightfall (for these were the longest days of the year), the women were startled by a great hubbub at the door, which resembled the hooting of children. In her curiosity and impatience Esther hastened to open the door, and discovered to her amazement, in the midst of a dozen or more boys who were throwing mud at him, a strange creature dressed like a gentleman but wearing the enormous head of an ass. The monster, who seemed either blind or intoxicated, bolted into the garden, slamming the gate behind him.

"Shut the door, quick!" muttered an indistinct voice which issued from the snout of the animal. "Can't you see they're hunting me?"

Mechanically the young girl obeyed, and then the intruder quickly removed his artificial head and displayed to the women the pale, haggard, dripping features of their friend, the music teacher.

"Mr. O'Flannigan!"

"O'Flannigan himself, astonished that he is still alive to tell the tale! Did you see those madmen?"

"Madmen! Why, the eldest was not more than twelve years of age."

"Are you sure of it?"

"Of course. But why this ass's head?"

"Well, they are having a terrible time with the Catholics this evening, and I thought it wise to be in disguise; and it's all right, since we are going to a masquerade ball. I hired from the property room at Drury Lane the ass's head which Bottom wears in the 'Midsummer-Night's Dream.' It fits me, does it not?"

"As if it had been made for you!"

"Unfortunately, in passing Charing Cross my chair was stopped and turned upside down by the populace, and my bearers deserted me like cowards. I hastily put on my ass's head, but evidently not quickly enough to avoid being recognized. I took to my heels, and they gave chase, screaming, 'Drown the papist!' and they would have been as good as their threat."

Esther burst out laughing.

"Bah! a parcel of children amusing themselves at your expense!" she said.

"Yes, children! For that reason I refrained from drawing my sword. Ah, had I had men to deal with, they would have paid dearly for their insolence!"

"You have indeed been magnanimous, Mr. O'Flannigan, which was worthy of you.—Now let us set out without further loss of time."

"But are the streets safe?" queried Mrs. Marsham.

"I believe it is all over. At least I hear nothing."

In fact it was the moment of cessation of hostilities when the rioters evacuated the Palace Yard.

Without accident a hired carriage conveyed the two women and their escort to Oxford Road, where the Pantheon was situated.

The passion for masked balls which had been the delight of the contemporaries of the first two Georges had received a serious check about the middle of the century, at the time that Europe was terrified by the report of earthquakes. London believed herself upon the eve of experiencing the fate which had befallen Lisbon. Indeed, a prophet appeared in the streets who announced the destruction of the city upon a certain date. On the night preceding the fateful day a great part of the population emigrated and encamped in the open air; but, though the dreaded event passed without catastrophe, a vague terror prevailed, paralyzing all sorts of pleasure. From their pulpits the popular preachers thundered against the vices of the day, and especially against the abominable license of masked balls. God was about to chastise England; already was His arm upraised against her. No more masquerades, or a rain of fire and brimstone would devour the new Babylon; the earth would yawn and engulf in its entrails the sinners, with their infamous tinsel and their masks, which hid all their impurities. Thus attired they would appear before their pitiless Master, and would pass from the laughter and intoxication of the dance hall straight into the inexpressible anguish of the last Judgment!

Thus at one fell swoop the masked balls disappeared.

By degrees, however, the panic calmed, was forgotten, and in time became a historic memory. The strong-minded even risked a smile at the recollection.

The first time that a purveyor of amusement spoke of resuscitating masked balls a wag remarked, "He may be going to treat us to an earthquake!" The proposition met with success, and the whole town hastened to the *fêtes* which Teresa Cornelys inaugurated at Carlisle House in Soho Square. In the first place, the good Cornelys asked no money; oh, no! If she accepted a little it was devoted to the purchase of charcoal for the poor of London, who were suffering extremely from the cold that winter. But the summer came, and still the dances continued at Carlisle House. The Cornelys explained that her aim was to encourage business, which was undergoing a crisis. (Business is always undergoing a crisis!) Nevertheless, the bishops complained loudly of the liberty which reigned at Madame Cornelys's house; according to them Carlisle House was a very bad place indeed.

It was then decided to create a masked ball, access to which should be refused to persons of questionable reputation, and to which only women of the fashionable world should be admitted. The Pantheon threw open its doors on the 27th of January, 1772. On the very first evening Miss Abington, who occupied a place in the foremost rank of the excluded, presented herself smilingly at the door, fluttering her fan with a victorious air.

"Mademoiselle," faltered the master of ceremonies respectfully, "it is with the profoundest regret that I am forced to refuse you admittance to this house. The rule is stringent and—"

Miss Abington turned and gave a signal, whereupon forty gentlemen in good order appeared, with drawn swords. The poor master of ceremonies yielded to number, and Miss Abington made her triumphal *entrée* to the ballroom. Through the breach thus opened passed the whole army of vice, from the princes' favorites to the rovers of Drury Lane.

The evening was well advanced ere Mrs. Marsham and her niece entered the great rotunda, both in domino and masked. Upon coming out of the fresh, sleepy streets through which their coach had jolted them they were dazed and overwhelmed at finding themselves in the midst of such a furnace and din. The confusion amounted almost to delirium. The atmosphere was hot, heavy, and charged with pungent perfumes. The heat was so excessive that the candles melted and ran down upon such maskers as were not upon the lookout. Fifteen hundred persons, some intoxicated, others excited by the stir, the fun, and the noise, talked, laughed, screamed, and fluttered about; while their feet raised a dust which rose in a cloud and spread like a fog, enveloping the entire scene. Such was the turmoil of the crowd that the strident scraping of the violins and the shrill blasts of the horns were only occasionally heard.

"This is Bedlam let loose!" remarked Esther.

"It is hell!" responded Mrs. Marsham, who trembled with emotion and already regretted having come to such a place.

Mr. O'Flannigan, who was stifling beneath his ass's head, scarcely seeing anything and hearing nothing, kept turning from one to the other of his companions, but he had not counted upon his prominent snout, which continually struck them in the face unless they dodged quickly.

Amidst the rout they soon began to distinguish certain details, certain characteristic figures. A sultana, half-naked beneath her diaphanous draperies, was borne in a velvet palanquin upon a cardboard elephant, the legs of which were formed by four stout men, conducted by a magnificent Mussulman with a long beard and a golden caftan, and with an enormous ruby in his turban. Two little negroes, one bearing a casket of perfumes, the other waving a fan of plumes, slipped into the hands of the gentlemen mysterious bits of paper carefully folded. Upon each of these was found the address of the merchant in Bond Street who sold East Indian stuffs at the lowest cash prices, and for whom the masquerades served as an advertisement. The *cortége* closed with a group of odalisques, in the midst of whom a grinning eunuch carried a banner upon which was inscribed, "Slaves for sale." These odalisques were perpetually assailed by a band of man-monkeys, who left nothing to be desired in the way of audacity and effrontery. Next a Friesland nurse-girl, her head covered with metallic ornaments, gravely carried a little dog in her arms swaddled like an infant. Then came a personage half-miller, half-chimney-sweep, one side being white with flour, the other black with soot. A rigorously straight line divided his forehead, followed the line of his nose, crossed his mouth and chin, and apportioned his body into two equal parts. Among the promenaders were to be seen a dark-lantern, an artichoke, the shaft of a pillar, an egg-shell, a gigantic spider, and a corpse swathed in his winding-sheet, carrying his coffin under his arm, which he showed to the ladies with a gesture of jovial invitation that was received with roars of laughter. Adam and Eve in flesh-colored tights with a cincture of leaves in painted paper carried between them a little tree, about the trunk of which was entwined a remarkable imitation of the serpent. As she passed along Eve gathered crystallized fruits from the tree and offered them to the men with a sweetly innocent smile.

Caricatures of living personages were also seen, and easily recognized and understood. A mariner's compass which bore a vague resemblance to George III. held its needle turned towards the north, that is, towards Lord North, who advanced in the garb of Boreas, having a hideous cannibal upon his arm,—the symbol of the alliance between the Prime Minister and the Indians. Another group, formed by a Spaniard, a French coxcomb dressed in the latest Versailles fashion, and a Virginian planter (the three enemies united against England at this epoch), fled before Dame Britannia, who lashed them soundly to the immense delight of the patriots in the hall. A woman impersonating Intrigue whispered mysteriously, distributed bags of money and pension certificates, and wore the national coat-of-arms, on which the horse of Hanover was represented as kicking the British lion, while she stamped with rage upon a ragged piece of paper upon which was written in large letters, "Bill of Rights." Near her the Pope, with mitre on his head, turned somersaults and juggled with Saint Peter's keys.

"We had better go above in order to have a bird's-eye view," said Esther to her aunt.

So they dragged poor O'Flannigan up to the top of the staircase, stumbling as he went.

From the upper floor, leaning upon the velvet railing, they viewed the spectacle for some time. The great rotunda seemed like the crater of an active volcano, while the vapor that ascended scorched their cheeks. At this moment a string of men and women, uttering insane cries, whirled round and round the hall with ever-increasing velocity. Woe to him who met them in their mad career! Woe to the one who fell, for he would be trampled under foot! Carried away by the intoxication of their folly, they regarded neither decorum nor obstacles, and in their wild sport lost the very sentiment of their existence as they whirled like gnats dancing themselves to death in the sunlight.

The two curious women turned away. Close about them were different scenes, other phases of pleasure. In adjoining halls, which represented, according to the fancy of the time, the interiors of Chinese and Japanese houses, persons seated at tables ate and drank. There were hungry women among them who greedily devoured pork-pies with prunes; others who nibbled cakes and sipped whipped cream. Champagne and Rhine wine flowed in torrents. From obscure corners came the sound of whispered words, stifled laughter, and the smack of kisses. Elsewhere the merry-makers made greater exertions, and the supper was changed into an orgy. Mounted upon a table a young girl of sixteen danced with a man's cocked hat slipping down over her eyes. Another with dishevelled hair had thrown herself upon a man's knee, tossed her naked arm about a second, and was smiling at a third with a glance languid, half unconscious with wine. Still another, stretched at full length upon a sofa, slept as tranquilly as if she had been in bed.

"Come away, quick!" ejaculated Mrs. Marsham, uttering mental anathemas upon her curiosity.

At this moment, in an alcove between two pillars, Esther perceived two persons,—a man and a woman, partially concealed by the draperies. The remarkable thing about it was that the latter wore a domino exactly similar to her own,—brown with blue ribbons. The man, leaning towards her, spoke in low tones, seeming to beseech, to supplicate her; while she, with a wave of her fan and a shake of the head, said "No" with a coquettish gesture,—that sort of a "no" which is the preface to and synonym of "yes." Undoubtedly it was one of those momentary love affairs which are born and expire by the myriad upon such nights. However, the cavalier appeared to be more serious than the men about him. The way in which he pressed one of the little hands which had been entrusted to his clasp, and sought to plunge his gaze through the openings in the mask to find the eyes of the unknown, was at once anxious, impassioned, and sorrowful. For one moment he turned his head, but in that moment Esther recognized Francis Monday!

98

The impression that she experienced was one of more unexpected violence than she would ever have been able to imagine or foresee. Every drop of blood in her veins fled to her heart, and her limbs trembled. Being dragged away by her aunt, she took several steps without knowing whither she was going. That one moment sufficed to reveal to her the fact that she loved, and to teach her at one and the same blow that he did not love her. She had permitted herself to believe his tender words, his sad glances, and the recital of his early hardships; it had seemed so sweet to console the lonely orphan. It was for him, without her daring to frankly confess it even to herself, that she would willingly sacrifice her dreams of fortune, grandeur, and pleasure! And Frank was a libertine, after all, like the rest of them; he had never even thought of her! At the thought her irritation against herself knew no bounds. The spirit of audacity and adventure, which had often tormented her, rose imperiously and urged her on, as the spur incites the high-bred horse.

"I have had a narrow escape," thought Esther; "a hut, a garret with *him*, the joy of freezing to death, of starving for bread! That is what I have been nigh to plighting my troth to,—I, a daughter of Shakespeare,—I, who was born for a brilliant career, for great *rôles* and lofty emotions!—The die is cast: I shall be Lady Mowbray!"

The two women with their ass-headed cavalier had returned to the foot of the stairs. All at once a woman flung herself upon O'Flannigan, uttering so shrill a cry that even amidst the deafening uproar more than thirty persons turned and paused to witness the scene which was about to take place.

"Wretch!" screamed the woman, "is it thus that you desert me, and our poor children crying for bread?"

"I!" faltered O'Flannigan, paralyzed with surprise, and well-nigh strangled by the stranger, who had seized him by his ruffled shirt-front.

"Yes, you! While you are promenading here with hussies, whom I should blush to touch with the tip of my finger, you leave your lawful wife to the care of the parish!"

"Madam, there is some mistake! Permit me to say to you, with all the respect due to your misfortune, that you hold me too tight! You will tear my ruffles, which belong to the property-room of Drury Lane. I repeat, there is some mistake!"

And taking off the ass's head, O'Flannigan revealed his honest face convulsed with perplexity. The spectators crowded anxiously about them.

"No, there is no mistake! You are, indeed, my husband, Pat O'Flannigan, music teacher and prompter to Drury Lane Theatre."

"Certainly, I am O'Flannigan, music teacher and prompter at Drury Lane, but as to being your husband, may Heaven confound me if I ever set eyes on you before!"

"You have never set eyes on me? You have never set eyes on Molly MacMurragh, to whom you were married by the priest at Bray, in Ireland? You have never set eyes on the mother of your six children?"

Mrs. Marsham loosened her hold upon the unhappy O'Flannigan's arm.

"Can this be true?" she cried. "Can this woman really be Mrs. O'Flannigan?"

"My dear madam, I protest! There is no Mrs. O'Flannigan! This woman is either a fool or a jade; she has been hired by my enemies!"

"A fool! a jade! If there is any jade here it is this bold hussy who has helped herself to other people's belongings, and seduced a married man from his duty!"

"Mercy!" gasped Mrs. Marsham in horror.

"I do not know," cried the woman, "what prevents me from tearing off her mask, and leaving the marks of my nails upon her as the headsman brands forgers!"

She advanced menacingly, and shook her clinched fist in Mrs. Marsham's face, who feebly cried, "Help! help!"

A circle had been formed; those who could not see elbowed their neighbors, or mounted upon chairs, while such exclamations were heard as—

"Two women! They're going to fight! Bravo! Let 'em go!"

Some one cried out. "I'll wager five to one on the lawful dame!"

To which came the reply, "I'll take you!"

Others made sport of O'Flannigan's piteous face. Mrs. Marsham had let go of Esther's hand, who found herself in the background, and quite unnoticed. Presently a voice close behind her pronounced these words very distinctly,—

"The moon is risen!"

She trembled in every nerve; her heart beat violently. Her whole future life depended upon the step she was about to take. In that supreme moment the pantomime which she had just surprised above stairs shot with the rapidity of lightning through her mind; again she saw Francis Monday pressing the hand of the unknown domino and supplicating her with his eyes.

"Enough!" thought she.

She closed her eyes as does one who is about to leap into an abyss.

A hand seized hers and drew her away, and without a word she followed her guide.

CHAPTER XIII.

MOWBRAY'S FOLLY AT CHELSEA.

The situation was becoming critical for poor O'Flannigan and his companion, when an unexpected ally appeared upon the field of battle, in the person of the majestic Oriental who had served as the elephant driver.

"Look here!" he cried. "This is a shameful farce. This gentleman is innocent; I'll go bond for him! And as for this brown-skinned Jezebel, do you not recognize her as the gypsy who told fortunes at Saint Bartholomew fair, and who has so often been hauled up before the magistrates in Bow Street?"

"It's a fact!" explained some one. "It is Rahab, the gypsy queen!"

"Call the watchmen and let the beggar be taken to prison!"

From all sides resounded groans of disapproval. "No, no! no police! This is a joke. Don't do her any harm!"

But at the words "watchmen" and "prison" the gypsy had folded her tent and silently stolen away.

Assisted by his generous auxiliary, O'Flannigan conducted Mrs. Marsham, suffocating with mortification and rage, to a retired seat in an almost deserted side-room. There a footman brought her a glass of water, of which she swallowed half and then proceeded to take a survey of her surroundings.

"I shall remember this evening!" she remarked. "The Lord has punished me for my curiosity as he chastised our mother Eve before me. However," added the good woman, relieving her mind with a fib, "I wished to give my niece the pleasure."

The words suggested the girl.

"But where is Esther?" she exclaimed.

"Sure enough!" said O'Flannigan. "What has become of Miss Woodville?"

Different suppositions were offered. She must have become frightened; she must have been separated from them by the crowd.

"But she must be sought! She must be found!" cried Mrs. Marsham.

"How was she dressed?" inquired the man in the turban.

Mrs. Marsham described her niece's costume.

"Useless to search for her. Miss Woodville has been carried off, or, rather, she has followed her abductor of her own free will. I divined that all this ridiculous rumpus had but one object,—to daze you and distract your attention. At the moment that I came to your relief I saw with my own eyes a brown domino with blue ribbons going towards one of the doors on the arm of a masked gentleman."

"Esther! It is impossible, sir!"

"I beg your pardon, madam. And I can go further: I can give you the name of her abductor."

"Who was it?"

"Lord Mowbray."

"As you seem to know so much," said O'Flannigan, "pray who are you yourself? A sorcerer or the devil himself?"

By way of answer the Oriental removed his false beard.

"Mr. Fisher!" exclaimed the Quakeress and her cavalier in the same breath.

"At your service. This is Prospero's beard in the 'Tempest.'"

"Well done!" said O'Flannigan. "The Shakespeare accessories have been largely plundered this evening! But tell us, Fisher, what leads you to suppose that Lord Mowbray has designs upon Miss Woodville?"

"I have had proofs enough," replied Fisher mysteriously; "all the proofs I want, you may believe me."

The hairdresser considered it unnecessary to say more, or to add that the proofs in question bore the effigy of his Majesty.

"Merciful Heaven! what shall I do?" cried Mrs. Marsham wringing her hands.

"You had better warn your son," suggested the Irishman.

The Quakeress quaked with terror.

"Reuben! He will overwhelm me with reproaches!"

"Never mind what he says. He is the betrothed of his cousin; he is energetic and courageous; if any one is capable of snatching the girl from impending doom, it is he. There is not a moment to be lost."

"But where shall we find him?"

"As to that," replied Fisher, "nothing is easier. All day long he has been at the head of the papal enemies. I must be greatly mistaken if he is not at this moment engaged in setting fire to the Sardinian chapel."

It was thereupon decided to place Mrs. Marsham in safety in Fisher's house, which was near Oxford Road, while the two men went in search of Reuben.

The hairdresser had friends everywhere. At the door he received fresh tidings which confirmed his suppositions. Capt. Hackman, Lord Mowbray's inseparable companion, had been seen in Oxford Road with a pistol under each arm. A carriage without armorial bearings, with neutral colored livery, had been stationed at a short distance. A masked gentleman with a brown and blue domino upon his arm had come out of the Pantheon. He had signalled the carriage, which had approached, and the man and woman had entered it. Thereupon Hackman sprang upon the box, saying to the coachman, "To Chelsea!" Then the horses set off at full speed towards the left, narrowly escaping running over people. There was still another version which a page had to tell. It was the same masked man and the domino in the same colors; only the affair had taken place at one of the little side-doors of the Pantheon. Instead of the coach a sedan-chair had carried off the fugitive towards the right, in the direction of the city. In affairs of the kind there are always points of difference among the witnesses. Who was to be believed? Evidently those who had recognized Hackman and heard the address given to the coachman. It was towards the "Folly" at Chelsea that Mowbray had undoubtedly taken his victim. Fisher was an alert and intelligent man. Some minutes later, divested of his turban, his Persian robe, and his beard, he joined Reuben in Duke Street. The vandals had achieved their work, and the crowd of by-standers, lit up by the flames, gloated over the spectacle. The blazing pile, formed of the ornaments of the chapel, was beginning to flag for lack of combustibles.

A horde of children of fourteen or fifteen years of age, having taken the places of the men, danced about the charred remains, uttering cries and causing a flame to spring up here and there by administering a kick to the embers. A transient glow illumined the street, revealing the faces of terrified women at the windows, and in an obscure corner a group of the rioters with their hats drawn down over their eyes. Among them stood Reuben, coldly implacable, watching lest any one should approach the fire to save or steal anything.

It was at this moment that Fisher approached him and whispered a few words in his ear. Reuben started in surprise and rage.

"Esther carried off by Lord Mowbray! Taken to Chelsea!" he gasped.

However, he quickly regained his composure and reflected for a moment.

"Friends," he said in a loud but firm voice, in order to make himself heard by the thirty or forty men grouped about him, "there is nothing more to be done here. If we remain longer we shall be hunted down by the soldiers, of whose approach we have already been warned. Let us disperse, to meet again within the hour at Chelsea, near the Bun-house. Thence I will lead you to the assault of a house, the master of which secretly favors the papists."

For the time being Reuben was falsifying; but examples in Holy Scriptures which authorized a pious lie crowded his memory. He also added in an assured tone, casting an expressive glance upon the band of pillagers who had given some sign of discontent,—

"This house is full of riches. It also contains a young girl prisoner, one of our own set, whom this villain has seized to make her the toy of his pleasure. Let us hasten if we hope to arrive in time to save her!"

These words were received with murmurs of adhesion. The little legion of disorder divided into groups, set off through the streets that led westward, and gained the place of rendezvous by different ways. Reuben accompanied Fisher, who recounted the details of the adventure as they went along.

The Bun-house was celebrated at the period for the fabrication of those somewhat heavy and substantial cakes which still form the traditional family diet on Good Fridays. In fine weather a goodly company was wont to wend its way thither for the purpose of eating buns and washing them down with port. When George III. passed that way, on his way from Kew to Saint James's, he did not disdain to stop and chat familiarly with Mistress Hand, the pastry-cook. She must have slept like a log that night not to have heard the strange assemblage which formed under the walls of her garden. Reuben found but a few of the fanatical sectaries whom he had led to Parliament. Weary with the fatigues of the day, content with having intimidated the representatives of the nation, as they flattered themselves, and destroyed two of the lairs of idolatry, they had undoubtedly gone home and to bed. One phrase only in Reuben's brief harangue had carried the day,—"This house is full of riches!" Well might he be astonished, for the words had fallen unintentionally from his lips. But if Reuben remained unmoved, Fisher trembled at sight of the bandit faces which surrounded him. Seeing them thus, no one would have suspected that these shady cavaliers were marching to the defence of menaced innocence.

All told, they were some forty men armed with pistols, clubs, and knives. Truly formidable, resolute, ready for anything, accustomed, as it appeared, to such nocturnal escapades, they marched silently, and obeyed promptly with some show of discipline.

"Yonder is the house," said Reuben, "behind those trees. It is best to form a ring about it so that no one shall escape us."

"I have been hostler at the Folly," said a red-headed fellow with a hang-dog look, advancing as he spoke; "there is a breach on the north side of the wall through which I used to slip every night to join my sweetheart Peg, who was maid at the Nell Gwynne. If it be your will, I will conduct you."

"Lead on!" answered Reuben laconically.

A few minutes later the troop penetrated the little park and crept softly in the shadow of the great trees, avoiding the gravelled paths. The thick sward muffled their footfalls, while a high, warm wind, which had arisen, rustled the foliage, thus favoring them by masking still more such sounds as they did make. Occasionally a pebble crackled or a dead twig snapped beneath their feet, but that was all. For the space of fifty yards about the house extended an open space.

"Halt!" whispered Reuben in a prudent tone.

The house was in complete darkness; it seemed either uninhabited or wrapped in sleep; however, upon examination Reuben and Fisher discovered a ray of light which filtered between the closed blinds upon the second floor.

"They are there!" thought Reuben, quivering with rage; while aloud he cried,

—

"Forward!"

They obeyed the command with a rush; but undoubtedly some one had been watching, some one whom they had not perceived. The alarm had been given, and the heavy oaken door, swinging upon its well-oiled hinges, closed in their faces. Then from within followed the sound of bolts being shot into place and of the adjusting of bars.

A pause ensued, a moment of amazement, and then an outcry of rage mingled with at least forty oaths. The man who had spoken before, the former hostler, again ventured to the rescue.

"Behind the laundry," said he, "there is a pile of lumber, placed there for the building of a summer house. With one of the rafters we could force the door."

Reuben approved the scheme. A few moments later an improvised battering-ram, borne upon twenty shoulders and skilfully balanced, at the word of command went crashing against the solid woodwork. At the third blow a splitting sound was heard.

"Listen!" cried Fisher. "Some one above is speaking."

The men, panting, and bathed in perspiration, paused.

In fact, a window upon the second floor had been suddenly thrown open, and a man—probably Lord Mowbray—had appeared upon the balcony. Every eye was raised to him and every tongue hurled some insult at him in the same breath. With a calm curiosity he regarded the crowd swarming and howling in the darkness beneath him.

"Gentlemen," he said, "we are at least a dozen strong here, well armed and determined to defend ourselves. The first man who sets foot within this house will pay dearly for his imprudence; but before we resort to bloodshed, suppose we hold a parley. What is your will with me? Do you fancy, perhaps, that I am a papist? According to my nurse I am a member of the Church of England, and I am ready to pronounce in your presence the test oath or any other oath, to swear by the body of Christ, the belly of Mahomet, by Belial or Beelzebub."

This harangue scandalized Reuben's virtuous friends, while it set their rowdy escort in a roar of laughter. Young Marsham was not slow to appreciate the *prestige* which such jocose coolness in the hour of his peril was giving Mowbray,—a supreme quality in the eyes of an English mob; therefore he hastened to interpose.

"You are detaining a young girl here whom you have abducted from her family," he declared.

"It is true," answered Lord Mowbray; "there is a young lady here. Do you wish to see her?"

"At once! I insist upon it!"

"I do not understand your last words, but I willingly yield to your request. Madam, be good enough to show yourself to these gentlemen, who are nervous about you."

He turned towards the interior of the chamber and bowing respectfully, with much grace extended his hand to a woman who stood there, and assisted her to step out upon the balcony. At the same time he added,—

"Hackman, my good fellow, give us some light."

Capt. Hackman, with a blazing torch in each hand, appeared upon the balcony in his turn.

"It is she!" cried Fisher. "I recognize the brown domino and the blue ribbons! I can swear that it was I who furnished that mask!"

"Madam," said Mowbray with renewed demonstrations of respect, "are you here of your own free will?"

The masked woman gave an affirmative sign.

"Has any one molested or offended you in any way?"

She answered by a negative gesture.

"Esther," cried Reuben, "can it be that you have forgotten—"

Mowbray quickly interrupted him.

"Come, come, sir! Is it in so numerous a company as this that one proceeds to indulge in a family explanation, or gives a curtain lecture to a young girl? Be good enough to come up here. You will find my house open to you, but to you alone. I give you my word that if, after some moments of conversation, you still persist in claiming this young lady, she shall follow you. On the other hand you must swear to me—"

"I never swear," said Reuben rudely.

"There you are wrong," retorted Mowbray courteously; "an oath frequently eases matters."

"It is written, 'Thou shalt not take the name of the Lord, thy God, in vain.'"

"Very well. But promise me at least that, during the time, your men shall not move or commit any folly."

"So be it."

And turning to his companions Reuben added, "If in the space of a quarter of an hour I do not come out of this house, enter and cut down with your swords whomsoever you may meet!"

"An admirable plan," concluded Mowbray, always ironical.

When Reuben, having been introduced into the enemy's camp under a flag of truce, had at last reached the apartment upon the second floor, Mowbray remarked:—

"Now, madam, you may unmask."

The young woman loosened the strings of her mask, and Reuben found himself in the presence of Bella, Lady Vereker, whose black eyes regarded him with a singular expression of mingled curiosity and amusement.

"You are surprised, sir," resumed Lord Mowbray, "as I was myself an hour ago. Heaven is my witness that it was not her ladyship whom I supposed I had carried off; but after all, as the French proverb has it, *Quand le vin est tiré, il faut le boire*, and an old sweetheart, like old wine, is best."

"Insolent fellow!" murmured Lady Vereker, toying with her fan.

Still Reuben remained sombre and defiant.

"What assurance have I," he demanded, "that this lady is not your accomplice?"

Then her ladyship with feigned anger mingled with raillery, exclaimed:—

"I! when I have wished my reputation to protect that of my young friend!"

Without pausing to consider this important sacrifice, Marsham continued:—

"And what assurance have I that my cousin is not concealed in some corner of this accursed house, for it is certain that she has disappeared?"

"If she has been carried off, it must have been by the devil," said Mowbray, "and unfortunately I cannot be held responsible. I freely consent to your searching the house. I can refuse nothing to so amiable a man."

Conducted by Hackman, and accompanied by Fisher and the former hostler, who knew all the ins and outs of the place, young Marsham visited every recess of the "Folly." Carrying to a grotesque degree the affected civility of his patron, the captain preceded them, opening all the cabinets, the wardrobes and the closets, and even inviting them to examine nooks scarcely large enough to stow away a hare in. Quite unmoved by his impertinence, Reuben and his companions sounded the walls with their sticks.

"Esther! Esther!" cried Reuben in a loud voice. But there was never a reply.

The officious Hackman, who stood aside at every door according to the rigid rules of French courtesy, showed them the kitchens, the offices, in fact everything, sparing no detail. He insisted that they should explore the entire length of the two subterranean passages, one of which led to the open country, the other to the river bank.

"Now," he remarked, "you know the house as well as its architect."

"Well?" inquired Mowbray of young Marsham when he returned from his fruitless exploration.

"I have found nothing, my lord," answered Reuben with a tinge of embarrassment.

"Then undoubtedly you divine what I expect of you."

"That I dismiss the men? I was about to do so." He stepped out upon the balcony and addressed his companions.

"The young girl whom I sought is not here; at least she is no longer here. Consequently your presence is no longer required and you may retire."

A muttering of evil augury arose from the ranks of the little group.

"These gentlemen will not go," suggested Mowbray, "until my butler has given each of them a half-guinea with which to drink my health. It would be a pity to give such brave fellows so much trouble for nothing."

A general cheer and cry of "Long live Lord Mowbray!" responded to this largesse.

"I knew," continued the young nobleman, "that we should understand each other. The manner in which you have split my door has given me a high opinion of your ability in case of an emergency, and it appears that we should accomplish great results, were I your leader.—Stay! There is, hard by, the residence of a papist, which ought to be sacked. I have a mind to lead you thither myself. It is not that I owe the papists any particular grudge, but I am ready to labor for honor's sake, and for the love of the art."

The enthusiastic cries burst forth anew. Reuben could not but feel that his day was over, and that henceforth Lord Mowbray was the true master of his men. With a haughty, sullen air he turned towards the door.

"I reserve my suspicions," he said. "We shall meet again, Lord Mowbray."

"One moment, if you please. I reproach myself with having concealed something from you. There is a chamber in this house which has escaped your examination."

Saying which, he moved a small picture and pressed an invisible button. One of the panels in the wainscoting shot upward without a sound, like the curtain of a theatre, revealing a narrow passage. Mowbray led the way, Reuben following him. After a few steps he found himself in a circular apartment furnished with extraordinary richness and taste. From the ceiling fell a rosy radiance, soft, tender, and faint, vaguely illumining the tapestries with which the walls were draped, upon which were represented rare subjects derived from Boccaccio. The feet sank into a rich carpet as into the sward of glades which no human step has ever pressed. The low rounded furniture seemed fashioned to render the fall of a body insensible and silent.

Ere Reuben had had time to cast his glance about the apartment the panel had fallen into place, leaving no more suggestion of a door than a wall of polished steel. Mowbray had vanished, and Marsham was alone. In an excess of rage he flung himself against the wall with all his might, he scratched it with his nails and beat upon it with his clinched fists.

Ten feet above his head a peephole opened, in which was framed the mocking face of Mowbray.

"You are giving yourself needless exertion," he remarked. "The panel will defy all your efforts. No one can hear you, and no one will release you before to-morrow morning. A night of seclusion in so charming a place is scarcely cruel chastisement enough for your insolence, more especially as this prison saves you from another. At this moment they are searching for Reuben Marsham high and low, but truly such a boudoir as this is preferable to a cell in Newgate. Therefore be resigned, and seek some means of passing the time. Ah, I forgot. You will find a venison pie and a bottle of Canary wine upon the table at your left.—And now, good night!"

And the peephole closed.

There was no timepiece in that strange boudoir to mark the flight of the hours. Naught disturbed the profound silence of the night save the cracking of the crystal sconces as one after another the candles expired. At last a feeble ray of the crescent dawn descended from the vaulted ceiling. In the numerous mirrors, which had reflected many a festal scene, Reuben caught a glimpse of his own haggard, watchful face.

CHAPTER XIV.

VAIN QUESTS.

The preceding events had occurred upon the night of the 2d and 3d of June. The next day, Saturday, the city was comparatively quiet.

A feeling of assurance pervaded all classes; once again it was believed that the riots were over. On Sunday morning several priests ventured to celebrate mass with closed doors before their little nervous congregations, who trembled at the slightest sound from outside and apprehensively watched the doors, thinking of the catacombs without possessing the courage of the early Christians. But on that same Sunday, in the afternoon, the disorders began again and increased until nightfall. On Monday matters were aggravated.

The blind fury of the rioters augmented with their number. It was now directed against the wealthy Catholics and such influential personages as had cast their vote in favor of tolerance. Savile House in Leicester Fields was assaulted and the proprietor, Sir George Savile, one of the most enlightened, amiable, and humane men of his time, nearly lost his reason and his life. The mob broke into the residence of Lord Mansfield, who escaped, half-naked, with his family, by the rear entrance. They then built an immense pile of his furniture in the street and set fire to it. Barnard's Inn and the Langdale distillery in Holborn yielded to the flames. Several entire districts fell a prey to the insurgent population. A dome of smoke hung over the city from Leicester Fields to London Bridge, which by night flared like a vault of flame.

However, no one seemed moved as yet. Curious idlers flocked to the scene. Between a game of "quadrille" and a sitting at the magnetizer's, the fair gamesters, with their idle, foppish escorts, arrived by the coachful upon the theatre of riot and conflagration. It frequently chanced that they were set upon and robbed, the men of their purses and snuff-boxes, the women of their watches and jewels. Sometimes the traces were cut and the horses sent flying off in terror, while the coach was tossed upon the blazing pile. Amidst all this the peaceful watchman passed with slow, methodical gait, appearing to see nothing, quite as if all were calmness about him, and swinging his sickly little lantern here and there in the blinding glare of the fires.

Whether through inertia or policy, magisterial authority moved neither hand nor foot. Col. Woodford having given his soldiers command to fire upon the mob, popular exasperation rose to such a degree that he was obliged to hide himself for several days. While the Guards were leading their prisoners to

Newgate they were assailed with every description of missile. One of them being wounded in the face and maddened by the sight of blood, was about to fire upon the crowd, when his captain exclaimed, "In Heaven's name, do not fire!" Such management as this made the fortune of the insurrection.

If any one considered that King George's ministers were cowards who had lost their heads, he was seriously mistaken. These gentlemen, with truly British phlegm, listened to the cries of "Death!" raised against them much in the spirit that Fielding, playing besique behind the scenes of Drury Lane, lent one ear to the public hissing his plays. The recital of an eye-witness describes some strange pranks during the sittings of the Council. He affirms that there was more claret discussed than resolutions.

"Though I," said Lord North, indicating his colleague with pretended terror, "go about armed to the teeth, I am more afraid of Saint John's pistol than anything else!" Thereupon they ascended to the roof of the house. Thence they observed the conflagration, noted its phases and progress, and exchanged conjectures upon the direction of the wind and upon its probable effects.

"And now, gentlemen," concluded the minister, "let us return and finish our wine."

This government, discredited on account of its external showing, cared not to assume the odium of an energetic repression. Curious as it may seem, it was upon the opposition that it sought to shift the responsibility. It was said that Lord North held an interview with Fox in the lobby of Drury Lane Theatre. A plenary reunion of the Privy Council was held under the presidence of the king, which only occurs at serious crises and in times of great peril to the monarchy. The judges were convoked in order to pass their opinions upon the course of procedure to be pursued and to give their advice upon the legal side of the question. It was Burke, the great Liberal orator, who proposed to proclaim the martial law.

In fact, the most alarming tidings were received hour by hour. The Fleet and Newgate prisons had been forced, and had vomited their prisoners upon the pavements of London. At Rag Fair and similar localities the orgy was at its height, the license of the mob unbridled. It was no longer a question of papism and tolerance: it was a social revolution, greatest of all misfortunes, which had begun; it was the subversion of law, the accession of crime. It was reported that a formidable army was forming for the assault of the Bank of England. Inasmuch as the bank was the vital centre, the very heart of the country, the ministers awoke from their lethargy. As if by enchantment several regiments entered London from all sides and encamped with their cannon in Hyde Park. A plan had been decided upon for the total annihilation of the revolt. Lord Amherst mounted his horse, and when by the ruddy light of the conflagration the aged courtier was seen advancing it was generally understood that that class of society, until now so disdainfully indulgent, had taken a hand, and would show itself pitiless in the defence of its property and life. Soon the firing resounded far and wide,—at Blackfriars, at Saint George's Fields, near the Mansion House; the victims lay about in heaps, while the Thames received many corpses and more than one living sacrifice.

On that terrible night, during which the horrors of civil war were added to those of incendiarism, while so many men animated by the spirit of vengeance and the hope of pillage rushed upon one another, a little band of kind-hearted folk, moved by so much suffering, patrolled the streets, bearing relief to the victims. It was Levet, the surgeon of the poor, who urged them on, and case in hand led that dangerous campaign in the interest of humanity.

As he trudged along Cheapside with his troop, who carried the litters and ladders, he recognized Francis Monday walking in the opposite direction, and called out to him,—

"Is that you, Frank?"

The young man quickly raised his head, perceiving his former savior, whom he frequently went to see and for whom he cherished a grateful friendship.

Perhaps it is time that the young artist's conduct at the Pantheon ball was explained.

As must have been already divined, he loved Esther Woodville—loved her with an exclusive, profound passion which was born on the same day that the girl made her appearance upon the stage of Drury Lane. Standing in a corner of the *parterre*, Frank had experienced those devouring sensations which have disturbed twenty-year-old hearts ever since the world began.

The passion which actresses inspire in young men of indigent circumstances and timid disposition is the most romantic and delightful of all, since it unites every impossibility and chimera.

The footlights seem an obstacle which it is impossible to surmount; possession appears an infeasible, madly absurd dream, the very thought of which produces vertigo. The unrecognized lover is not jealous of the comrades who elbow his idol and speak familiarly with her; he does not even consider the admirer or husband who awaits her behind the scenes. They find in her but a woman like unto all other women. The mistress of his heart is in his sight Juliet, Imogen, Ophelia, Desdemona. She imparts her youth and beauty to the *rôle*, lends poetry and passion to it. From such a *mélange* is born a perfectly adorable creature who only exists for a few hours for the public, but continues to live for the lover long after the curtain has fallen and when the actress has washed off her paint and is supping with a hearty appetite.

In this fashion had Frank loved Miss Woodville until the day that he had met her face to face in Reynolds's studio. From that moment the young girl replaced the artist in his mind, and he fell to loving her in another guise. Their lengthy chat on the day that Sir Joshua was absent from the studio had for the time being awakened certain hopes in his heart. Why should he not love her? Why should she not grow to regard life with his eyes? Little by little, however, without the slightest event interposing to undeceive him, he realized how poorly calculated were his modest lot and unceasing struggle with poverty to tempt a girl reared amidst adulation and covetousness, amidst circumstances which could not fail to nurture her vanity and her taste for luxury. \Many times had she returned to Sir Joshua's, and each time she had addressed him some few rapid words, always with a touch of embarrassment, —annoyed, as he fancied, at the recollection of that hour of freedom and intimacy, desirous perhaps of effacing it from her memory. The thought smote him to the heart, and, though accustomed to the slings and arrows of outrageous fortune, resignation came hard.

Proportionally as the great painter advanced in his work, Frank secretly copied the portrait of Esther. One morning, while busily engaged at his task, the source of mingled pleasure and pain, a light chuckling caused him to start suddenly and turn.

"You accursed gypsy!" he cried, turning pale with anger, "who permitted you to enter here? How dare you spy upon me?"

It was Rahab, who, together with her numerous vocations, joined that of model, and frequently posed for Sir Joshua. More than once, annoyed at the procrastination or laziness of his fair clients, the painter had set the head of some patrician dame or artist upon Rahab's beautiful body, a genuine living manikin whom he could pose and drape according to his fancy. Rahab had also consented to pose for Frank; and, although she professed disdain for Christians, her hard, ironical eyes sometimes softened as they rested upon the young man.

To-day she was not stirred by his anger, but with a shrug of her shoulders remarked:—

"Poor boy! She will never be yours."

"Why not? Tell me, since you pretend to read the future."

"Because she loves Lord Mowbray."

And, turning upon her heel, she danced away, humming some gypsy ditty.

That name filled the boy's soul with discouragement. Lord Mowbray! A cold-hearted libertine, the most corrupt, 'twas said, of all the Prince of Wales's new *coterie*. And it was towards him that Esther's heart had been attracted! And the passing sympathy which he had inspired in her was due, perhaps, to his resemblance to that man! His grief was profound; he had experienced nothing akin to it since the day in his babyhood when he had lost his precious goldpiece.

Revolving these facts in his mind, he had gone to the Pantheon. Why should he go to a masquerade? By what sentiment was he actuated? Some vague desire to console his aching heart by a vulgar adventure? The hope of meeting Esther there? No: rather that instinct which sometimes impels the downcast to air their woes in the midst of a crowd. And while he stood absently watching that wild scene, that dance of fools, a hand was laid upon his shoulder.

Rahab again! What would she with him, this compatriot of the Sphinx, with her fathomless black eyes and enigmatical smile?

"The one you love is here!" she breathed.

"What! Esther?"

"Brown domino with blue ribbons. Seek and you shall find. Is not that what you say?"

"Yes; but explain."

"The moments are precious. In a few minutes Esther will be lost, lost forever. Hasten, if you wish to save her. In saying this I betray some one whom I ought to serve, but I am a woman and I pity you."

He would have questioned her further, but she slipped away and vanished among the groups of maskers.

As deeply moved and agitated as he had just been indifferent and discouraged, Frank traversed the ballroom, searching in every direction for the domino which had been described to him. All at once he uttered a stifled cry; he had discovered the object of his quest. He hastened forward and was at her side in a moment. She was alone, but her eyes, seen through the openings in her velvet mask, seemed to be anxiously watching.

"Esther," he said to her, "a danger menaces you. What it may be I know not, having only received a hint of it: but permit me to follow your footsteps that I may watch over and save you; for save you I must in spite of yourself."

He had seized the young woman's hand and was pressing it between his own, without for a moment doubting that the true Esther stood before him.

The unknown answered never a word, but yielded her hand to his clasp as though she derived some pleasure from the contact with this feverish love. A man approached them and for an instant raised his mask. Frank recognized him; it was Lebeau, Lord Mowbray's intimate companion. The young man turned upon him with a menacing air, determined to prevent his companion from following him.

"Is your ladyship ready?" inquired Lebeau.

"Quite ready. Good night, Mr. Monday."

The voice of Lady Vereker! Frank remained riveted to the spot in amazement. So, then, the gypsy had tricked him. He left the Pantheon and gained his lonely garret room, vainly seeking some solution of the adventure.

Next day Mr. Fisher did not appear, as was his custom, in order to serve Sir Joshua. However, the riot had ceased, and to all outward appearance London had regained her wonted tranquillity. Soon it would be known that Mr. Fisher had passed the night searching for Miss Woodville, who, according to report, had been carried off by Lord Mowbray. The accident was of too common occurrence to arouse spirited comment, especially at so serious a time. The invasion of Parliament, or what almost amounted to an invasion, was an affair of far greater importance than the abduction of an *ingénue*. On this account Ralph, who gayly recounted the news to the young artist, was stupefied to see him seize his hat and rush forth into the street.

Frank hastened directly to Fisher's house, who had at once shut himself up in prudent reserve; but, pressed by questions and touched by the young man's emotion, he ended by narrating the night's events and proposing that he should call upon Mrs. Marsham. The good woman had wept incessantly and was in a fine frenzy of despair, having fallen from a state of the most serene confidence into the extreme of despondency. Her niece abducted; her son lost to sight but sought by justice for the events of the preceding day, of which she was beginning to comprehend the importance; her house occupied by soldiers; and even Maud gone, no one knew whither nor with whom! Such a conglomeration of misfortunes was indeed enough to disturb the steadiest brain and unseat the best established optimism. It was amidst such disorder that Frank found her, ignorant how to solve the problem, and fearing, if she claimed the aid of the authorities to find her niece, that by the step she should deliver over her son to his hunters.

There was no help to be expected from this poor, half-crazed woman; Fisher had his clients to attend to; while O'Flannigan, believing himself menaced as a Catholic, remained under cover in his lodgings. Thrown upon his own resources, Frank registered a mental oath that he would find Esther, and during those days of terror and battle, indifferent to the prevailing trouble, insensible to his own danger, he came and went, passing from the turbulent quarters to the more peaceful districts, searching the lost clew with impassioned despair.

From the first day he knew beyond peradventure that Mowbray's "Folly" was deserted. Thanks to the persuasion that resides in a goldpiece, the footman who was left in charge of the place found no difficulty in permitting the young man to enter. He showed him all the secrets of the house, the subterranean passages, even the boudoir where Reuben had passed the night.

"At daybreak," said he to Frank, "the stranger and the young lady were placed in a berlin, and no one knows whither they went."

Frank was satisfied by Fisher's recital that "the young lady" could have been none other than Lady Vereker. It was she who had mystified Mowbray as she had for a moment deceived him. She, then, was the one to give him the key to the enigma. He hastened to her residence, but was not received. Her ladyship was not in town! He recalled the gypsy's words, who, undoubtedly having been paid by the young nobleman, had played a part in the comedy. In order to find her he visited every spot where the gypsies were accustomed to camp, —Blackheath, Hampstead, the fields adjoining the Edgeware Road and Notting Hill. All in vain! Probably the members of the tribe had rushed into the thick of the riot which occupied the heart of the city.

At last he understood that the gypsy had been but an instrument. As for Lady Vereker, would she be likely to wish to save Esther or recapture her lost lover for her own sake? Would she not play her own game? Would she obey the will of the one who had directed the whole intrigue? It was then that his thoughts reverted to Lebeau. That mysterious person who was said to be the purveyor of Lord Mowbray's diversions had always inspired him with a vague repulsion. Two or three times he had met him, and each time he had felt annoyance at the piercing glance which the man had fixed upon him. Still it was he who had approached Lady Vereker at the Pantheon and had asked,—

"Are you ready?"

Frank began to suspect some shady machination to which Lebeau held the thread.

While Lord Mowbray, accompanied by his faithful Hackman, was seen everywhere, following with the interest of a dilettante the progress of the riot, Lebeau was invisible. Where was he concealed, and why should he conceal himself? Was Esther his prisoner, the victim of this scoundrel in some undiscovered lair? Frank's blood curdled with horror and rage at the thought.

It had been reported that at the moment Lord Mowbray's coach had carried off a masked woman, another young woman similarly attired, and escorted by a gentleman whose features were not distinguishable, had entered a sedan-chair which stood in waiting for her at one of the side entrances. This chair had been borne off rapidly in the direction of the city. Frank had questioned every chairman he chanced to meet; no one could or would give him the slightest satisfaction. After three days of fruitless search in every sense, he was at last forced to avow his impotence, when he was accosted by Levet, the surgeon.

"Come with us," said the big-hearted man; "there are Christians to be succored, lives to be saved, for to-night the devils are loose, and I know not which are more to be feared, the incendiaries or the soldiers. Since so many are doing their worst, let us try to accomplish some little good."

Without a word Frank followed him. He needed action to lessen his fever, to make him forget his mortal anxiety. The office which he was about to fill at Levet's side was rife with peril, but whenever did a desperate man count the cost of his action?

CHAPTER XV.

SANCTUARY.

That same night, in a poorly furnished chamber, Esther sat, with bowed head, and hands clasped in her lap. By her side crouched an aged woman who mumbled incessantly, mingling wails, maledictions, and incomprehensible reminiscences of her childhood with fragments of prayers and scraps of biblical texts. She spoke to herself, never addressing the girl, who on her part paid her no heed. Esther's attention was riveted upon the sounds which reached her from the streets. With every minute the firing of a platoon, the crash of a wall undermined by the flames, or a savage clamor which rent the air, reached her ears and made her tremble.

The chamber was situated upon the second floor of a low house at the end of an alley, apparently deserted by its inhabitants; for there was no movement of life and no human being in sight. But at sixty paces away, though invisible, the great artery of Holborn, filled to overflowing with the howling, maddened crowd, sent a rumor of its infernal tumult to the two women. No candle burned in the room, but the neighboring glare from the conflagration of Langdale House illumined every object as distinctly as though it were noonday. Thus the hours dragged themselves away in gloomy monotony, notwithstanding the proximity of the confusion and the fury of human passions in a state of paroxysm. Suddenly Esther sprang to her feet.

"Maud," she exclaimed, "the flames are gaining upon us!"

It was true. From the side of the little court upon which the chamber looked, the panes of a grated window had burst into fragments, while a tongue of flame had suddenly darted forth, licking the blackened walls and casting its lightning athwart the pervading flare.

"Maud! Maud! Soon it will be no longer safe for us to remain here!"

"God be praised!" answered the old woman, having raised a vague glance upon the scene. "He gives the victory unto his saints; it is he who has cast both horse and rider into the sea!"

"She is madder than ever," thought Esther; "this night has quite unseated her reason.—And Mons. Lebeau does not return!"

What was to be done? What resolution ought to be taken?

The circumstances which had led her into this perilous situation passed swiftly through her mind. When she had placed her hand in that of the unknown who had pronounced the preconcerted signal,—"The moon has risen!"—she immediately experienced a sense of regret at her fault; but this regret had not been sufficiently potent to arrest in time the accomplishment of her resolution. She permitted herself to be conducted to the door where the sedan-chair awaited her.

"No!" she then exclaimed, "this is enough! I will go no farther!"

"This is no time for discussion," replied an imperious voice which was not Lord Mowbray's; "get into the chair, quick!"

The thought of Frank, whom she was now certain she loved since jealousy had cast its unerring ray into the depths of her heart—this thought tortured her.

"I am lost!" she cried, "lost!"

"On the contrary, you are saved!"

And with the words ringing in her ears the chair started. The men almost ran with it, the result of the masked personage having said something to them about "paying double."

In less than a quarter of an hour the chair stopped in an alley-way off Holborn, and the gentleman, conducting the fugitive into one of the houses, dismissed the bearers.

When at last they were alone in the chamber upon the second floor and the man had succeeded in lighting a candle upon the mantelpiece, Esther easily recognized him.

"Mons. Lebeau!" she gasped in surprise.

"Yes," he replied, "and you are out of all danger here, absolute mistress of your destiny, since all that I wish is to offer you some respectful advice."

"But how could you have known? How could you take the place of another?"

"That is my secret—at least for the present. It is enough that I have succeeded. One word which has escaped you has led me to believe that you will not blame me for my intervention. I await the assurance with anxiety. Have I been in the wrong to act as I have?"

"No," she answered after a moment's hesitation, "and I thank you. I do not love Lord Mowbray, and my folly was as inexcusable as it has been without consolation."

An expression of joy illumined Lebeau's withered features.

"Good!" he said. "But what motive has led you astray for the moment?"

"Vanity. Lord Mowbray assured me that he wished to make me his wife."

"His wife! He never dreamed of doing such a thing! Moreover, such a marriage would have been impossible. But let us speak no more about it."

"Are you not going to take me back to my aunt, whom I left in such a ridiculous predicament, and who must be dying with anxiety about me?"

"The predicament of which you speak must have soon terminated; and as for her anxiety, it is my duty not to disturb it for the present. Lord Mowbray has sworn that, by consent or force, he would abduct you this night, and I am not sure that you would be safe in the house in Tothill Fields, where there is no one to defend you, not even your cousin Reuben. These are my humble lodgings, although none of my acquaintances know of its existence nor the way thither. Rest here for a few hours. To-morrow, by daylight, we will consider the situation. Be very sure that Mrs. Marsham will raise no objection, will address you no shadow of reproach. Your fault will not transpire, since I will tell her that it was I who brought you here to save you from the peril which menaced your honor."

"She knows you, then?"

"Very well indeed."

"For some time?"

"For a very long time."

After a brief pause he added,—

"It was I who brought you, a little child, to her house before you were confided to the care of the Quakeresses at Bristol."

"Is it possible!"

And, impetuously seizing Lebeau's hand, she added:—

"Then you knew my parents? O, I beseech you, sir, tell me something of my mother! Who was she? Do I resemble her? Where did she die, and how?"

The queries crowded to her lips in an imperative tumult.

Lebeau's features relaxed in a melancholy smile.

"Patience!" he replied. "Later I will tell you all. Only know that your mother was exceedingly beautiful, and that you are her living image. She too was carried away by excess of emotion and by the thirst of adventure. There was no one at hand to give her timely warning, and she paid dearly for her imprudence."

Esther bowed her head, while a tear glided slowly from her lashes to her cheek.

"It was then that your father met her and took pity upon her. She was in sore need of pity and protection. Her child was born. You are that child."

"Alas!" murmured Esther. "But my father—is he still living?"

"Yes."

"Why does he not come? Why does he not show himself? I should be so happy to embrace him!"

At this moment an extraordinary change took place in Lebeau. His features, scarred by the battle with life, his dulled eyes, his entire vulgar face were ennobled with a solemn tenderness. Irresistibly his arms seemed to open to clasp the girl to his breast. Then they fell at his sides, and his face resumed its expression of discouragement and fatigue.

"Your father would indeed be happy," he said, "and very proud to call you his daughter; but circumstances prevent. I do not justify his conduct; far from it. He has committed wrongs, grievous wrongs,—and even more than that!"

Esther recoiled from him violently.

"You are my father's friend, and you calumniate him!"

Lebeau's only response was a shrug of his shoulders and a sigh. He turned to the window, and from a convulsive movement of his back Esther divined that he was weeping. In a moment she was at his side.

"Pardon me!" she cried, "pardon! You are perhaps the only human being whose interest in me is not tainted with calculation. You have saved me from death, you have saved me from shame, and by way of recompense I accuse and wound you! O, pardon me, my friend!"

Delightful words to Lebeau's ear!

"Thank you, my child," he said; "thank you, and good by. It is already daybreak, and all is calm. Sleep in peace. In a few hours I will return."

And Mons. Lebeau hastened away. Left alone, Esther dared not undress in a house which filled her with forebodings. She threw herself upon the bed just as she was, clasping in her hand a tiny poignard which had been Garrick's gift. Tradition had it that the weapon had once belonged to Sir William Davenant, who pretended to have received it from Ben Jonson. The latter, while a soldier in Flanders, had purchased it of a Jew who came from Italy. It was a marvellous bit of Florentine work, and must have been manufactured towards the close of the fifteenth century. What had been its history? In what dramas had it taken part? What ferocious jealousies, what mortal desires, had it served? Had it ever been dyed in human blood? In whose snowy breast, in whose throbbing heart, had it been plunged? Considering these fancies, but especially her own destiny, her imagination in a whirl, our little heroine fell asleep.

When she awoke she perceived Lebeau, who stood watching her as she slept, and she heard the clocks chiming high noon.

"Well?" she demanded.

"I came from Tothill Fields," he answered; "the house is full of soldiers come thither to arrest your cousin Reuben, and they are to remain there, lying in ambush to surprise him upon his return. Your aunt has not come home, and up to the present time I have been unable to discover her place of refuge. Old Maud was alone at the mercy of the soldiers, whom, in her turn, she provoked and insulted. I have brought her here. She will attend to your wants and will be a companion for you so long as you are obliged to lie in concealment here, which from present appearances may be for some time; for the city is still in an agitated state, and this very disorder singularly favors your admirer's plans, since he has not lost the hope of taking his revenge."

Soon after Lebeau departed, promising to return on the morrow with the latest tidings; but Sunday passed and he did not appear. On Monday a child brought an unsigned note from him, which ran:—

"I cannot come to see you. I am suspected, and every step I take is shadowed. Have patience until to-morrow."

The rioting had begun again, and the two women in their sanctuary listened to the sound of it as it grew each minute more distinct. Esther slept but little that night.

Next day affairs assumed an even more threatening aspect. The Langdale distillery was in flames close by, although the situation of the house prevented the girl from following the progress of the catastrophe. Towards evening, when the tumult increased and the firing became general, her agitation was extreme. The sight of the flames which enwrapped the neighboring buildings and threatened her refuge put the finishing touch upon her anxiety.

"Shall I remain here," she thought, "shut up with this crazy old creature, who does nothing but sing psalms? Shall I suffer myself to be burned alive in this strange trap? Mons. Lebeau has forgotten me or else he cannot come to me. Who knows if he is even alive?"

She approached the window and looked at the tower of St. Giles, upon which the clock marked the first hour of a new day. So brilliant was the flare from the conflagration that Esther could distinguish the delicate V-shaped shadow which the hands made upon the dial, the slightest detail in the sculpture about the dial, and even the joining of the masonry.

She resolved to depart. But where should she go? She knew not; but first of all it was necessary to escape from the circle of fire which was fast hemming her in. She put on her mantle and cast a silken handkerchief over her hair, knotting it under her chin. Then she called Maud, who had passed into an adjoining chamber.

But here she found herself in the presence of an unlooked-for difficulty. The old woman had fallen fast asleep and only responded to her words, her entreaties and cries by vague mutterings without awakening in the slightest degree. Esther shook her in desperation and tugged at her garments, but her girlish strength, depleted by the sense of her peril, was powerless to arouse the inert mass.

Perhaps she might secure assistance from outside! She opened the outer door, and, standing upon the threshold, cried, "Help!"

All in vain; her voice was lost, incapable of piercing the tumult. She was scarcely able to hear it herself. No one appeared. The neighboring houses, deserted as they were, were slowly yielding to the flames, and no one appeared to think of disputing the ravage. The almost intolerable heat fairly scorched the girl's eyelids.

Then she rushed towards Holborn, crossed like a flash the vaulted arcade, the only exit which opened from that side, and ran into the highway.

There she paused, terrified by the spectacle which met her gaze.

———————————————

CHAPTER XVI.

GAMES OF DEATH AND CHANCE.

The Langdale establishment, changed into a furnace, belched forth torrents of fire at every aperture. The roof had fallen, and the flames ascended free of all impediment in one great sheet, which, being lashed by the wind at a certain height, curved into an arch and threatened to deluge the city with a devouring rain. Before the vast blazing pile a hideous, anomalous mob clad in indescribable rags and tatters, danced with furious, drunken joy. Several hours earlier the great hogsheads which had been dragged out of the distillery had been knocked in the head without ceremony, and every one had drunk his fill. Then the precious liquids had escaped, forming foaming pools and rippling rivulets, in which rare old port mingled with malmsey, and gin with sherry. Along the line of these pools and rivulets a crowd of human beings of both sexes and all ages, some with their infants in their arms, crouched upon their hands and knees, stretching their lips to sip the wine and mud. These were very soon rendered incapable of regaining their feet and insensible to the brutal passage of fresh bands, who trampled them under foot, and thus increased the quivering heap. At last the sparks falling from the lurid heavens ignited this sea of alcohol, which surged in bluish, spectral waves, enveloping the wretches, drowning while it set them on fire. The wallowing bodies writhed like mutilated serpents, the spasmodic convulsions, vain, desperate efforts, and hoarse cries having in them no semblance to humanity. Thus the most horrible of deaths fell upon them in the midst of their intoxication, without so much as sobering them in the moment of dissolution. Meanwhile the rest, amidst all this horror, continued their demoniacal dance.

One of these fiends espied Esther. Staggering with open mouth and outstretched arms, hideous in his bestial carouse, he made two or three steps towards her. She fled back to the house, which she reached in a few moments. Upon the threshold stood Lebeau.

"At last!" she gasped. "I thought I was going mad!"

"Be calm," he replied. "I have found Mrs. Marsham, and I am going to take you to her. I know a way, but there is not a moment to be lost. In less than an hour this house will be reduced to ashes with the rest."

"But Maud!—she has lost her senses and refuses to follow me."

Without a word Lebeau hurried into the chamber, where he found the old woman. During the moment of silence that ensued Esther heard a sound upon the lower floor of the house.

"Some one has opened the door!" she cried; "some one is entering below!"

She thought with terror of the wretch who had followed her, and whom she had seen stumble over some obstacle and fall heavily to the ground, whence he was unable to rise.

Lebeau reappeared in answer to her warning of danger. Too late! Some one was mounting the stairs, advancing with rapid step, and when at last the flare of the conflagration fell upon his features through the open doorway Esther and Lebeau recognized Lord Mowbray.

The first thought that presented itself to the girl's mind was that she had been betrayed.

"Oh!" she cried, bending upon Lebeau a glance of despair and hatred, "you have ruined me!"

This fresh shock proved too much for her endurance. Exhausted with emotion, she fell, striking her head upon the foot of the bed, and lay there motionless upon the floor. Lebeau sprang to her, raised her in his arms, and placed her gently upon the bed; then he bent above her pallid face.

"Swooned!" he murmured, as if speaking to himself.

With folded arms Lord Mowbray watched him, following every movement with an ironical smile.

"Master Lebeau!" he said, breaking the silence.

"My lord?" answered Lebeau, turning and facing him, pale but resolute.

"Do you still deny that you have played me false?"

"More than ever do I affirm that I have served your lordship faithfully."

"By thwarting my plans and robbing me of this girl?"

"By robbing you of this girl, yes. It was my duty."

"Your duty? That is the first time I have ever heard the word upon your lips."

"That was my fault. After all, my lord, perhaps there is a God."

"You should have sooner told me so. If you are converted, go join the hypocrites of your ilk, and leave me. This deserted place, this night of conflagration and slaughter, this unconscious girl,—all suits me well. I have a fancy for adventure which has no vulgar tang about it."

Standing between the bed where Esther lay and young Mowbray, Lebeau did not move.

"Excuse me, my lord," he said steadily, "it is you who are to leave. You will not lay a finger upon this child."

"Why not?"

"Because I forbid you."

"And pray why do you forbid me?"

"*Because she is my daughter and your sister!*"

For an instant Mowbray stood transfixed with amazement; then he burst into a laugh.

"By my soul!" he exclaimed, "my father was right: you are the most amusing rascal in the world! Long live Lebeau! No human being but you could have conceived such an idea. The day that my father awoke in the bottom of that monster pie, the surprise was good, but it cannot hold a candle to this one! After this night's affair no one can ever say that you are degenerating; for your imagination, my dear man, was never so brilliant. Ask me a hundred pounds, or twice that amount; I will refuse you nothing. But go away now and let the farce end. I have enough of it."

"I shall not go, and this is no farce. I repeat, Esther Woodville is your sister."

The young man smiled disdainfully.

"Would you have me believe that Lady Mowbray—"

"Lady Mowbray was a saint! May she hear and pardon me!"

"Amen!"

"Mock if you will, for you will not mock long. Lady Mowbray had nothing whatever to do with this affair; moreover, Lady Mowbray was a stranger to your birth, sir!"

This time the young nobleman recoiled in rage.

"Listen to me," said Lebeau authoritatively.

Esther was beginning to recover a vague consciousness. Athwart the shadows of her swoon thought began to reassert itself, though doubtful, timid, misty. Stretched upon the bed, incapable of movement, her eyes closed, she heard voices without comprehending what they said, without distinguishing the sense of what was spoken.

"Twenty-three years ago," continued Lebeau, "two women were *enceintes* at the same time, the wife and the mistress of Lord Mowbray, one at his residence in St. James's, the other in a chamber of his 'Folly' at Chelsea. The latter was the daughter of a London shop-keeper, whom Lord Mowbray had abducted from her family, and had concealed as his prisoner. It was Fate's decree that his lordship should be made a father twice in one and the same night. He called my attention to your vigor and vitality when you came into the world. 'Look, Lebeau,' he said to me, 'it is a genuine love-child. See how strong he is, while the other—' Then a thought occurred to him: why not substitute the illegitimate for the legitimate child? He hated his wife as he hated all things good and pure. The thought of rearing the child of a rival charmed him, and he considered me worthy to execute the change. It was I who bribed the young nobleman's nurse and placed you in his cradle. When your mother's health was re-established Lord Mowbray washed his hands of her and the child whom she believed hers. It was enough for him that the child should be dispossessed of his fortune and title; he desired that he should be wretched, deprived of everything. He knew that the family of his mistress, inflexible as they were in principles, would close their doors upon the fallen girl and her child. At rest upon this point, he forbade me to give the sufferers aid, and I disobeyed him."

"That was the beginning of virtue!"

"No, sir. I found her beautiful and provided for her. In my turn she made me a father, but I treated her as though I were a grand gentleman. I sank to the infamous level of Lord Mowbray. I exposed her to all the hazards and misery of a wandering life. She became an actress and travelled from country town to country town, with a troop of mediocre actors, dragging Lady Mowbray's son along with her, the child whose position and name you had usurped. She died —almost starving!"

Lebeau pronounced these final words in a harsh tone of profound woe, upon which slowly accumulated remorse had set the tinge of indescribable bitterness.

"My daughter," he continued after a pause, "I saved from this cruel existence, provided for her education, and placed her in the home of honest folk."

"And the other,—the vagabond, my pretended brother?"

Beneath Mowbray's apparent irony Lebeau detected his anxiety.

"His life has been hard, frightfully hard, sir; until the age of ten years so cruel was it that the recital of his sufferings would touch any other heart than yours. From one adventure to another he at last fell into the hands of the Thames pirates, who made a little thief of him, and reared him for a life of shame and crime."

"Very much as you reared me."

"It is true. I merit the reproach and accept it; but while your evil instincts grew apace, the germ of good developed in your brother. He fled from those who had marked him for wrong-doing, and was received by upright persons. —Ah, you would like to know if he still lives? Do you think me fool enough to deliver him over to your jealousy and suspicions? No. You now know enough of this business to understand that you ought not to remain here an instant longer."

"I have listened to you even unto the end with a patience that astonishes me. It would appear from this recital that I am under nameless obligation to you, your *protégé*, your creature. As the king reigns by the grace of God, I am a nobleman by permission of Mons. Lebeau, and if I cease to merit his good opinion, I lose everything! Well," he added, suddenly changing his tone, "I do not care to know how much truth there is in your story, but I do know that this situation is no longer tenable. No such man as I am ought to be at the mercy of a Lebeau, hanging upon his discretion. The surest means of my assuring myself of your silence is to kill you! And kill you I will!"

Saying these words, he whipped out his sword and darted upon his former tutor.

Esther uttered a feeble cry, but the cry was lost in a frightful crash. A neighboring wall, undermined by the fire, reeled and fell, striking upon the roof of the house. A rafter in falling struck the window and shattered it. A dense, stifling smoke, starred with a myriad sparks, filled the chamber.

Meanwhile Lebeau, who had never for an instant lost sight of Mowbray's movements, had darted backward a pace or two, thus placing a table between himself and his adversary, at the same time drawing his sword in his turn. Now they were equally matched. It was he who had first placed a fencing-foil in the young man's hand, he who had taught him with infinite patience all the secrets of the French and Italian schools of fencing. In those very schools had they studied the noble art in company, not disdaining the lessons of resident masters. They had fenced together every day for ten years, but had never succeeded in scratching each other, so easy was it for either to parry the thrusts of the other and to divine his intentions. However, it was necessary that one of these two men, who had lived so long together as master and disciple, almost as father and son, should take the other's life; and each bore written upon his very eyes the fierce desire, the implacable longing, to kill.

It was not a duel, but a combat. Shifting their footing, retreating precipitately or lunging unexpectedly, profiting by every obstacle, bending forward until they almost squatted upon the ground, or bounding into the air, every few moments they would desist, watching each other, panting, bathed in perspiration, their features rigid as if petrified with the same mortal intent. The furniture lay about them upset and broken, and all the while the smoke continued to thicken. It grew suffocating and darkened the chamber, recently so bright, while at the same time it altered the character of the combat, which threatened to become a blind struggle in the dark. Not a word was exchanged; nothing was audible but the stifled oaths, the short, harsh breathing that rattled in the throat, the hissing of the crossed swords, that metallic sound which freezes the marrow in the bones like a death-knell. In the adjoining chamber old Maud chanted:—

"Saul hath slain a thousand, but David hath slain ten thousand! Glory be to the God of hosts! *Deus Sabaoth! Alleluia!*"

Outside the house the tumult of the horrible fête had waned and expired in a vague, distant wail, intermingled with the dying shrieks of the participants.

Slowly Esther raised herself upon her elbow; with eyes dilated with horror she watched the two men as they pursued and evaded each other, leaping like stags in the ruddy smoke which was neither day nor night. She fancied herself the dupe of some hideous nightmare.

Neither of the combatants seemed aware of her presence, since both held their sight riveted upon the tips of their swords as if their very souls had passed into the glittering points. But Lebeau was weakening, and he knew it. His grasp trembled and his sight grew dim from minute to minute. A cold sweat pearled upon his brow, which he attempted to wipe away with a swift gesture of his left arm; but the beads grew more abundant, dripped from his eyebrows to his eyelids, and obscured his vision. His weary feet struck the furniture; already had he stumbled once; a sort of vertigo caused surrounding objects to whirl about him. It was death!... Then in sheer desperation he thrust out blindly.

Esther saw the two men run each other through, fall almost one on top of the other, roll heavily over upon the floor, and lie motionless. Again she lost consciousness, and for a time no sound disturbed the silence of the chamber save the chanting of the mad woman.

However, Lebeau raised himself, and strove to collect his ideas and strength. He was losing great quantities of blood, but the welfare of Esther was the only clear thought which remained amidst the baleful giddiness which had invaded his brain. Save Esther! But how? Bear her away in his arms? He could not do it. Had he even the strength left to crawl to the stairs, drag himself down and through the alley in search of help? Yes, there was no alternative. But in the mean time would not the fire reach her in its swift course? Would not the smoke asphyxiate the poor child? Stimulated by this alarming thought, the unhappy man began to drag himself by his bruised and bleeding hands. Every now and then he was forced to pause, exhausted, fainting, believing that the end had come. "Esther!"—that name alone revived him. His daughter! his child! No, he would not leave her to die like that. As for himself, what mattered it? But *she*, so young, so beautiful,—she, for whom life was so full of promise! Thus he advanced step by step, lowering himself from stair to stair amidst the most atrocious agony.

But when he reached the foot of the stairs he discovered that the wind had closed the door which Lord Mowbray had left open. He stretched out his hand and tried to raise himself upon his knee. He could not do it. Horrible mockery! So simple an action,—to raise a latch, thrust open a door; but he could not do even so much, he who had accomplished such extraordinary feats! And salvation lay beyond that door, for it seemed to him—or was it an illusion?—that he caught the sound of voices in the court. He strove to raise his voice, but no sound issued from his lips. Then he sank down in an inert mass, his body obstructing the door which he would have given the last hour of his existence to open!

Lebeau had not been mistaken; there were voices in the alley-way. Perhaps, had he been able to attempt one supreme effort, he would have recognized the voice of his compatriot, the surgeon of the poor, and that of Francis Monday.

In fact, they were continuing their work of succoring the unfortunates, upon which they had been engaged for several hours. They had relieved more than one wounded sufferer, had snatched from the flames more than one wretch lying at death's door. They pursued their course like soldiers of duty and humanity, soiled with blood and mud, their eyelashes singed, their clothing in disorder. Many times had the flying bullets grazed them. Many times had they been insulted and menaced. They had seen one of their number crushed by the fall of a blazing wall, but their zeal had not been dampened; and it was Frank who, in a sort of heroic frenzy, now urged on his companions.

It was rumored in the crowd that behind the flaming ruins of the Langdale establishment was a group of dwellings, now wrapped in fire, which had not been evacuated by the inhabitants.

In seeking a way to reach these unfortunate sufferers, Levet and Frank had gained the alley-way upon which Lebeau's little house was situated.

Suddenly Frank paused.

"Did you hear that?" he exclaimed.

"What?"

"I don't know.—A voice—singing—in this house!"

They held their breath, and the psalmody of old Maud distinctly reached the ears of the surgeon and his followers.

"There is someone in there!" cried Levet, "and the roof is already on fire! They must be raving maniacs!—What ho! Within there!"

He walked around the house, endeavoring to attract the attention of the inmates.

"Can you not see that the fire is gaining upon you?" he cried. "Come out, quick!"

But there was no reply, only in the interim of silence they again heard the old fool's monotonous chanting, the very words even being audible.

"We must save them at any cost!" exclaimed Levet. "Come, comrades!"

They tried to force the door, but as it resisted their efforts they supposed it must be locked.

"To the window!" said Frank.

With a blow of his elbow he shattered the glass, and, inserting his hand through the fracture, adroitly opened the casement. It was one of the talents taught him by his early instructors, the river thieves.

Then, springing upon the window ledge, he entered the chamber, followed by Levet.

"One dead already!" cried the surgeon. "Great Heaven, it is Lebeau! No, he still breathes! Hand me a lantern, gentlemen!"

He was already upon his knees beside the dying man.

At the name of Lebeau a sudden thought crossed Frank's mind. If the man he had sought high and low had been found in this sordid retreat, perhaps he was close upon the solution of the enigma. Hastily he sprang up the steep steps of the little stairway,—so hastily that he slipped in the tracks left by Lebeau's bleeding hands. Upon the landing of the second floor an unexpected enemy lay in wait for him; a jet of smoke and flame, issuing from the wide-open door, scorched his face and nearly suffocated him. With his hands upon his eyes he attempted to rush through, but tripped over a pair of legs extended upon the floor.

"Still another body!" he thought with horror.

Upon his knees he felt his way with difficulty up to the face of the dead. It was Lord Mowbray who lay there upon his back, his hair burned to a crisp, his features blackened but still set in that last defiant grimace.

Frank had seen enough and was about to recoil to the door, when it seemed to him that in a corner of the chamber he descried a human figure lying upon a bed.

Gathering all his energy, he darted thither.

Esther!—it was she!

"Help!" he cried; "help! Levet!"

The surgeon answered the call with several men, but they were arrested by the terrible current of scorching air which traversed the chamber from the window to the door.

"She is dead, and I will die with her!"

Such was the only thought that filled Frank's distracted brain. In despair he threw himself upon the bed, murmuring, "Esther, my beloved!"

And even in that awful moment when his lips touched that still warm cheek the supreme contact was one of ineffable sweetness. Knotting his arms about the object of his love, who had not been granted the opportunity to love him, the poor boy bade farewell to life.

But simultaneously a voice, scarcely more than a sigh, murmured in his ear, "Save me!"

In an instant he was upon his feet. With a vigor of which he would not have believed himself capable a moment before, he raised the girl in his arms and sprang with her through the belt of igneous smoke.

CHAPTER XVII.

HORACE AND SHAKESPEARE.

The sun was already high above the horizon when at last Lebeau opened his eyes. The brilliant light of dawn, penetrating the chamber where he lay, wounded his sight, and his heavy eyelids drooped. After a moment he raised them painfully and perceived the kindly face of the surgeon of the poor bending above him.

"Do you recognize me?" he asked.

The sufferer made an affirmative sign and feebly faltered Levet's name. Then in a low, indistinct tone he inquired,—

"Where am I?"

"At Dr. Johnson's house. Keep perfectly quiet and all will be well."

Suddenly memory asserted its sway.

"Esther!" Lebeau cried, in as eager and anxious a voice as his utter prostration would permit.

"Miss Woodville is here. She is alive, having only fainted. There was a slight abrasion of the flesh behind her ear, probably the result of a fall; but that will soon disappear. And as for you, my good friend, we shall soon have you upon your feet again."

Lebeau moved his eyes in a negative sign, and with a sad smile murmured,—

"My account is settled. Why do you attempt to deceive me? Am I a coward?"

A moment later he asked,—

"Who saved Esther?"

"Francis Monday, the foundling, Sir Joshua Reynolds's pupil."

Levet briefly recounted how the rescue had come about; how old Maud, whose obstinacy and madness had nearly been the cause of her young mistress's death, had finally saved her life by her psalm-singing; with what infinite difficulty they had entered the house and snatched from the devouring flames three living beings and one corpse.

"One thing is certain," he concluded, "and that is, that these two children love each other. It was his future wife whom Frank saved last night in Holborn, and, though this sad week will leave its mark in ruins for many a day, it has at least served to make two hearts supremely happy."

A profound satisfaction overspread the pallid features of the dying man.

"Miss Woodville has begged several times to see you. Shall I bring her to you?"

Lebeau's face brightened still more. Then he appeared to reflect. Of course it would have been balm to his departing soul to make himself known to her, to be a father for one short hour, to go with the pardon and caress of his child. But would she not repulse him? Would she find him worthy of her? And after all, was it not better that she should remain a foundling rather than be known as the child of Lebeau, the adventurer, the professor and purveyor of vice to the great?—Ah, well! he would hold his peace, would die without disturbing any one, and leave her happy. But in any case he must hasten to inform Frank who he was, and give him the means of establishing his identity.

"Frank!" he murmured. "I wish to see Frank—to speak with him."

"You have made sufficient effort for to-day. Rest now; to-morrow you shall talk with him."

"To-morrow—I shall not be here. Go—go and find him."

Without further objection Levet, who understood the true condition of his patient, left the chamber. In a few moments he reappeared, followed by Frank and Esther hand in hand. Their faces, radiant with youth and happiness, clouded with sadness. With bowed heads and faltering steps they approached the bed. Frank paused upon one side, while Esther sank upon her knees at the other.

"Father!" she breathed.

"Then you heard—"

"All!"

The emotion proved too much for the sufferer. He felt his head swim, and believed that the final vertigo had come.

"Only one moment!" he murmured, as though demanding respite of the destructive forces of nature; "Frank must know—"

"Frank already knows that he is the true Lord Mowbray," whispered Esther.

"But the proofs!" pursued Lebeau; "the proofs are necessary. The nurse, Elizabeth Hughes, still lives—at Bangor—in Wales. She will give all the necessary evidence.—Elizabeth Hughes—do not forget!"

He was exhausted with so much speech. His aching eyes had lost their circumspection. Gropingly his hand sought the fair head of his daughter and rested there. Then his thoughts fled backward over forty long years. Again he saw the humble peasant's cot in the mountains of Dauphiné, whence he had set out to see the world. We saw a dying woman lying upon her bed,—his mother! Her faltering hand was laid upon his boyish head, pressing it gently, tenderly. All the remainder of his existence had vanished; all that remained was the Alpha and Omega; an utter void united that caress received and this caress given. It was a foretaste of that world where there is no reckoning of time, where moments are as ages, where thoughts and acts are lost in one eternal present.

Entering noiselessly, Levet passed here and there about the room upon tiptoe. Lebeau realized all that took place, but the power of perception had abandoned him.

"Are you there, doctor?" he asked.

"Yes."

"Bring them close to me."

Esther stooped and kissed the brow upon which the dews of death had begun to gather.

"We shall meet again, father," she whispered.

"Perhaps," faltered Lebeau.

"Did you wish to sleep?" inquired Levet, when the young people had left the room.

"No, but I could not die before them. There is no use in saddening their young lives."

The surgeon did not attempt to deny the danger.

"You are a brave man, comrade," he said; "and since you are able to look death in the eye, do you not wish to make some preparation? There is a Catholic priest here in the house. Although Dr. Johnson is no friend to the papists, he has given this man the protection and shelter of his roof. If you desire to see him I—"

But Lebeau made a negative sign, while by some singular reaction the sceptic and philosopher again took possession of his expiring body.

"Read to me," he said, "the ode of Horace—to Posthumus."

"Horace's ode to Posthumus!" repeated Levet, scarcely believing that he had heard aright.

But he had made no mistake. It was Lebeau's wish that the Horatian ode should be read to him instead of the prayers for the dying. The aged surgeon arose and passed into an adjoining apartment, which contained Dr. Johnson's library. Soon he returned with a large book in his hand, and seated himself at the bedside. In a slow, impressive voice he began to read the famous ode, which the dying man accompanied in a low murmur, punctuating the familiar verses as though he were giving the responses to a psalm.

"'*Visendus ater flumine languido*,'" Levet read.

"'*Cocytus errans*,'" continued Lebeau faintly.

But when Levet pronounced the fatal words, which typify "the end-all here," *Linguenda tellus*, he perceived that no response came from the bed. Quickly he bent above the poor pagan, and placed his hand upon his heart; finding no answering throb there, with reverent fingers he closed the eyes of the dead.

After a few days London regained her habitual aspect. Blackened ruins; fragments of walls and roofs, still sheltering emptiness; gaping, desolate spaces, which had once been human abodes with happy firesides, about which many generations had been warmed and cheered,—these alone remained to tell the tale of that four days' madness, of the strange delirium which had fallen upon the great city. But how many human remains lay beneath these ruins, which would never be recognized, and how many corpses had been swallowed by the Thames? One knew not, one dared not attempt to estimate. Some unfortunate wretches, who confessed nothing and remembered still less, or, lost to all sense of decency, accused each other, were hastily tried and hanged. The principal criminal, he who had loosed the passions of the populace, Gordon, was already under lock and key in Newgate. Had he been more misguided than perverse? He was given the benefit of the doubt. His madness, and perhaps his rank, saved him: but the remarkable fact remains that this man, who had set fire to London and led to death several hundred human beings, not to mention the enormous destruction of property of which he was the cause, was not punished; though a few years later, having written some insolent lines upon Queen Marie Antoinette, he was thrown into prison and there languished for the remainder of his days.

When Reuben at last appeared after a considerable lapse of time, the events of June, 1780, had begun to be obliterated from the public mind. Though in no way apprehensive for his personal safety, he seemed pursued by a memory, haunted by a remorse which it was impossible to evade. Gloomy and humiliated, he shunned meeting his "brethren," who accused him of having deserted them in the hour of peril. He made no opposition to his cousin's marriage, but refused to be present; and on the very day that the wedding was celebrated he embarked with some emigrants bound for Canada. Thence later he journeyed to Botany Bay, after which time no tidings were received from him. It was thought that he preached the gospel in Australia. Some believed that he was killed and devoured by cannibals; others pretended that he died at Sydney in extreme old age.

Lady Vereker, whose name has been assumed out of respect to her family, continued her disorderly course of life and became a desperate faro-player, remaining steadfast to her alliance with Lady Buckinghamshire, Lady Archer, and Mrs. Hobart. She transformed into a *quatuor* the ignobly famous trio whom the caricaturist Gillray so frequently exposed to ridicule and shame in his cruel sketches.

Mrs. Marsham recovered her peaceful afternoons in which she was wont to dream those pious dreams which translated her to Paradise, where she never failed to be received with distinction. Mr. O'Flannigan, the crisis over, resumed the slaughter of his enemies (in words, be it understood), and acted as prompter until his own cue came summoning him from the field of service. Maud never recovered the minimum of sense with which Heaven had endowed her. In the asylum to which she was banished she continually narrated the end of the world, which she firmly believed she had witnessed.

Thanks to the testimony of Elizabeth Hughes, Frank was able with but little difficulty to establish claim to his title and possessions. The king and queen, together with the entire nobility, evinced the deepest interest in his romantic story and that of his young wife.

He resolved to destroy the "Folly," which could only serve evil purposes and recall unpleasant memories. Before its demolition Esther expressed a wish to see the place which had exerted so strange an influence upon her life and that of her husband; consequently they visited those haunts which had never witnessed a pure, upright love,—love as clear as the day and conscious in its pride.

It was just one year after Lebeau's death, and a perfect summer's day. The radiance of an unclouded sun flooded the apartments, to which still clung an indescribably sensual perfume, the faded hangings, and licentious pictures. Esther could not disassociate the thought of her ill-starred mother from this abyss, while Frank evoked the memory of his mother, the pale, charming being whom Reynolds had sketched, towards whom his heart had involuntarily yearned. Had not every stone in this hideous house weighed upon her as heavily as though she had worn it about her neck? Had not every infidelity which this den of infamy had witnessed cost her a tear, a pang, humiliation? Thus, hand in hand, they passed from room to room, oppressed at heart; and they experienced a sense of infinite relief when at last the doors of the accursed mansion closed behind them and they saw God's daylight resting upon the meadows and the mellow cornfields softly swaying in the June breeze.

At the Bun-house were congregated many Londoners, who had come out to the country to enjoy this rare day. Sedan-chairs, coaches and horses held by pages in brilliant livery, formed a picturesque group; while dogs barked joyously amidst the crowd. The porters and grooms were grouped about a juggler, who aroused their merriment with his tricks, or smoked their pipes beneath the ample, pillared veranda of the house. Within doors some were admiring the silver pitcher presented to Mistress Hand by Queen Charlotte, or the two leaden grenadiers, with their German shakos in sugar candy, and uniforms of 1745; while others, seated about a grass plot beneath elm-trees trained into the shape of vaulted arches, sipped a dish of tea with one of those famous smoking, piping hot buns as its accompaniment. These delicate, savory confections had made the reputation of the house.

The remaining few had formed a circle about Rahab, the fortune-teller. Perceiving Frank and Esther among her audience, she impudently exclaimed, —

"Ask that pair if I do not tell the truth! It was I who predicted their happiness."

"You!" said Esther, amazed at her audacity. "Do you pretend that you

143

predicted to me—"

"I told you that you would marry Lord Mowbray. Have I deceived you?"

Esther smiled and blushed.

"Give her a trifle," she said to her husband.

And while the young nobleman emptied his purse into the gypsy's hands, Garrick's pupil murmured these verses of her favorite poet,—

> "All yet seems well; and
> if it end so meet,
>
> The bitter past, more
> welcome is the sweet."